HAPPILY
Married
HAPPILY
Divorced

I0666888

HAPPILY *Married*
HAPPILY *Divorced*

SWATI KUMARI

Srishti
PUBLISHERS & DISTRIBUTORS

Srishti Publishers & Distributors
Registered Office: N-16, C.R. Park
New Delhi – 110 019
Corporate Office: 212A, Peacock Lane
Shahpur Jat, New Delhi – 110 049
editorial@srishtipublishers.com

First published by
Srishti Publishers & Distributors in 2019

Acknowledgements

As I began to think of all those who I wanted to thank for their support, suggestions and hard work in making this book possible, the list continued to grow.

A million thanks to…

First, my wonderful readers, who have shown their loving support for my work and who continue to be a source of inspiration for me.

My husband Prabhat Ranjan, for his unquestioning support, unconditional love, laughter, and just plain fun!

My family and all my dear friends throughout the world for always being there to support me through all the ups and downs in my life, and for being my companions in the thrilling expedition called life.

With the subject matter of the book being so sensitive, I was under all the more pressure to get it right. I thank Auri for his time and feedback on Mitash's story, which ultimately forced me to re-mould it to become a better, more accurate account.

Bhawna Agarwal, Nandith, John Upchurch and Lohith for reading the first draft of the novel and giving your first feedback and encouragement.

Prof. Sridhara Murthy, Marie Helen Abbo, Alok Sarkar, Kirti Kohli for the motivation to take the road to reach my dream destination and being a constant support.

Stuti, Arup Bose and Srishti Publishers for bringing out the best in my words and making this book a reality.

The Honeymoon Couple

This particular Tuesday evening, Varushka was at Amsterdam Airport Schiphol. She had collected her boarding pass, dropped her luggage, completed immigration and security check. Now finally at the boarding gate, she waited for her British Airways flight to Delhi.

There were still thirty minutes left to board.

She took out her mobile phone from the outer pocket of her red handbag, and typed a message: *Will be there for the reunion on Thursday.*

She sent it to Nishav and locked the screen to a blank. Then, as an afterthought, she turned the screen on again, and checked in on Facebook: *'At Schiphol Amsterdam Airport, travelling to Delhi, India.'*

She slipped the mobile phone back into her bag.

The call for boarding was soon announced. Varushka picked up her handbag and a big backpack to join the queue of boarding passengers.

During the flight, she adjusted her bags in the overhead bin, and took her seat next to a window, resting her head on the back.

She took out her mobile once again to check for any messages before switching it to flight mode. A chill ran down her spine as she took a deep breath, closing her eyes.

Varushka's eyes were still closed when she felt someone tapping on her shoulder.

The warm touch, and a soft voice, brought her back to her senses.

"Excuse me, ma'am?"

She opened her eyes to see a newlywed north Indian girl, with her palms and forearms decorated with *mehendi* and red *chooda* adorning her wrists.

She returned her polite smile.

"Ma'am, would you mind exchanging your seat with one of our seats?" she asked, pointing to the corner seat in the middle row.

Varushka glanced in the direction and realised the couple would have to sit separately if she did not change the seat.

"My husband… well, if you are okay with it?" she said again.

Varushka complied.

"Yeah, sure. Why not!" she said with a smile before picking up her bag. The girl helped Varushka after signaling to her husband with a thumbs up.

Varushka and that man exchanged a glance.

"Thank you, ma'am," the man said.

"Have a pleasant journey!" she replied with a weary smile.

After a long wait, dinner was served. Then the cabin lights were dimmed as the passengers prepared to sleep.

It was late night Dutch Standard Time, but there was no sign of sleep in Varushka's eyes at all. All the movies had already been watched. Resting her head on the back of the seat, she turned to her left. A satisfied smile ran through her lips.

The honeymoon couple was in deep slumber, snuggling with each other.

Varushka closed her eyes with satisfaction, knowing that in the morning, she would be a world away.

The Get-Together

It was Friday evening and Varushka was about to reach Nishav's home. She had been very excited all morning as she was going to see her gang of five after seven long months.

Kesha, Arshiya, Nishav, Aniket and Varushka had been best buddies in college and played the role of bosom buddies who were genuinely interested in everything that happened in each other's lives. They knew everything about each other.

After college, all of them got pretty much involved in their routine lives. One day, they found out that Aniket and Arshiya's families had finally agreed to accept them as family. Nishav was returning from Australia. Everybody was excited for a reunion planned at Nishav's home in Gurgaon. The 20th of December 2017, they had decided.

On the intended date, Varushka was ascending the stairs to the second floor of Nishav's bungalow. It was about six in the evening when Varushka rang the doorbell thrice before his mom opened it and shouts of, 'Hayyyy.... Oooooo.... yaaayyy... finalleeeeee!' welcomed her in. Arshiya, Aniket and Kesha had already arrived.

While they made themselves comfortable on the sofas in the drawing room, Varushka asked about Nishav's whereabouts. His mom told her that Nishav was not home yet and his mobile was out of reach.

"And he asked us not to be late," Arshiya said looking at her as they all laughed.

For the next hour or so, the four of them talked, laughed and made fun of each other while eating snacks, without waiting for Nishav. Meeting old college friends after seven months was so crazy and exciting that they didn't even realize they were at someone else's place where they should display social etiquettes. Moreover, they had often been there, so they knew Nishav's mom very well. For the four of them, Nishav's house was a second home.

After a short while, the doorbell rang again. Varushka got up from her couch to open it.

"*Nishavvv!*" Aniket shouted, getting away from the dining table.

They all stood up to welcome him, and as soon the hugging session was over, they continued their meal as Nishav joined them.

After lunch, they moved to the third floor of his bungalow. This was Nishav's deck and was reserved for his friends. They were laughing at one of Aniket's jokes as they went up, and were still laughing as they fell on the king size bed and the giant couch in his studio room.

That night, the five of them in that room had an amazing time, talking about their past and present – about those lectures which they had bunked together, about the mission assignment nights, about their experiences abroad, and so many other things.

"So finally, we all are here again after seven long months!" Kesha said excitedly.

"And all thanks to the 'A square' couple...." Nishav added, hugging Aniket tightly. They all burst into laughter once more.

"But seriously guys... finally, how did your families agree? It was really a surprise when Nishav told me about your wedding, and then Aniket called up to confirm and invite me. Fortunately, I had already booked my ticket," Varushka said turning to Arshiya and Aniket.

"*Agreed?*" Arshiya, who was lying on the couch with her head on Aniket's chest, sat up all of a sudden.

"Then?" Varushka asked as the others looked on.

"You know that we dated for four years and now wanted to get married, despite years of trying to convince both sets of parents who were dead against this interfaith marriage," Arshiya replied.

"Four months back, we came to know that Arshiya is up the duff. Last month we exchanged the vows in front of the lady with the blindfold," Arshiya pointed towards her little baby-belly pooch as Aniket explained.

"SHIYANI is ArSHIYA plus ANIket," her chubby cheeks turned scarlet as she whispered.

"Now, along with our families, we are first going to my native place in Jodhpur and then to Arshiya's home in Hyderabad to celebrate our union."

"Oh my god… really?" Everyone looked at Arshiya in surprise and screamed with joy.

"Let's raise a toast for the newlywed couple and soon to be mommy and daddy!" Nishav cried as he reappeared with a few Cranberry Bacardi Breezers.

"Cheeers to Arshiya, Aniket and Shiyani!" they all screamed together.

The shades of the sky faded, and tinted from blue to orange and red to a darker hue of blue. The sunset brought a chilly breeze along. By now they had shifted to the terrace where Nishav had already arranged the mattresses with cozy blankets and a bonfire to compliment the magical evening of the Famous Five.

"So, what's your future plan?" Arshiya asked, looking at Nishav and Kesha.

"Planning to switch my job. Got an amazing offer from McKinsey Deutschland," Nishav replied excitedly.

"I am asking about your marriage plan, guys. See, Varushka got married. Aniket and I declared our wedding publically. Now only you both are deprived of this amazing experience," Arshiya clarified.

"Oh! Marriage? First, there should be someone to marry, right?" Kesha said.

"Then what are you waiting for? Ask your parents to start hunting. They will queue up a long line of perfect bachelors for you to choose from," Nishav said, stretching his arms wide open.

"Have you gone crazyyyy? I cannot think of this at all," Kesha said jumping over the couch.

"Why? What's the problem?" Arshiya asked.

"Varushka also had an arranged marriage," Aniket added.

"Then why did you both elope to marry the love of your lives?" Kesha said. "Marrying the one you already know influences love, trust and harmony better," she added.

"Ooooo... guys see. Someone seems to be badly infected with the love virus. So who is that unlucky guy?" Nishav teased Kesha.

"No one yet, guys. But I want to marry someone whom I know already, someone who understands my personality and I understand his. Since we would already know each other well, there will be no question of dowry between the families, or the notion that the daughter has to be sold off. I think there are lesser chances of conflict, and while some amount of disagreeing does happen, when all's said and done, the love between us will be celebrated, acknowledged and honoured. He and I will act as a salve to comfort each other's hearts. It is bliss to live with someone you already love," Kesha paused for a breath.

"In an arranged marriage, I sense constraint in one's opportunity of meeting a perfect lifetime match, decreasing the horizon of one's search within one's own caste and sub-caste," Kesha replied, inhaling the fresh chilly air, and seemed intoxicated by the thought of being in the arms of her fictional love.

"I don't know about your family, but my parents are going crazy. How long can I fight them? So I've admitted defeat. I have consented and asked my family to start searching for a bride for me. I doubt that I will ever fall in love and approach any girl with a proposal, or that a girl will propose to me. So, the easiest way of keeping everyone happy is that my parents arrange my marriage. I have no option right now. Love marriage is not my cup of tea," Nishav said.

"But don't you think that your parents will make you choose one among few of the options they will be getting through relatives? You will end up marrying on the basis of her looks, her parent's ability to buy you, or her degrees. Or that someone would agree to marry you for the salary that you're receiving in Euro and Dollar, or your family's property, and of course your boyish looks. Would it really guarantee a happy married life?" Arshiya asked.

"Sorry, Arshiya, but do love marriages guarantee that?" Nishav asked.

"A marriage is a gamble and made in heaven. However, the probability is higher in love marriages!" Varushka answered.

"An arranged marriage can be as successful or unsuccessful as a love marriage. Sometime ago, I was reading an article based on a research survey report which stated that the global divorce rate in arranged marriages was 6 percent approximately. A significantly low number, don't you think? Hence I rest my case as I don't think love marriages and arranged marriages are as different as we make them out to be by stereotyping them," Nishav debated.

"If a wedding is a tie that connects two hearts, then love is that cementing element that supports and makes that bond stronger. Think of cozying and snuggling together with your spouse, and looking back at your life together. You will have so much to look back upon – the moment of your first meeting, falling in love, the proposal, and finally when you committed your 'I' to turn to 'we' and got married. It is a feeling of pleasure and thrill of two hearts committing to be one – friends into lovers that no arranged marriage can match, no matter how much 'love' the couple in the marriage has. Married life becomes a voyage that you relish when you are married to your love. Moreover, you will always strive and do your utmost to improve. You know the person better and know how to handle and adjust to be happy and make your marriage happier. All thanks to the love you share with your best friend, spouse and lover," Arshiya said.

"Then those adjustments can be made in an arranged marriage as well. At least, there won't be any pre-perceived expectations. People change after love marriages," Nishav objected.

"People do change with time. No matter if it is in a love marriage or an arranged one. What if looks, or the financial situation changes after marriage? Time is never constant for anyone. I support love marriage," Ankit said.

It is better to go for something with a higher probability of success unless you are looking for too much of adventure in life," Varushka said.

"While the modern wisdom of the millennial finds itself more inclined towards love marriage, a significant amount of marriageable individuals choose to go the good old arranged way in India. Irrespective of the privileges an arranged marriage offers like family support, there are definitely some benefits of marrying someone for love. Well, this has been a topic of heated debate since eras. But tell me one thing, what would you talk with your first date arranged by your family? 'Can you cook? What can you cook?' Errr… this sounds like a chef job interview. 'Do you keep your room clean and organized?' Oops… now this is like someone is interviewing a prospective maid. 'Are you a virgin?'" Aniket tried to change the debate that was getting too personal for his liking.

"Oh yes, and I would be happier if she says 'no'. I would thank god that at least she is modern, intelligent and opinionated," Nishav commented.

Everyone burst into laughter.

"Guys, we have an expert here. Varushka, what were the topics of discussion when you met him?" Kesha asked, looking at Varushka.

"Don't ask her. How could you forget that she fought with the guy in their first meeting itself? That guy refused to meet any girl after that," Aniket said trying to be funny.

Quickly adding on before the girls ganged up on him, "Enough about love marriage vs arranged marriage." He blushed in embarrassment.

"Varushka, we all are sharing our adventurous stories, what about you? How is your handsome hunk of a hubby?" Arshiya asked.

Nobody said anything for a few minutes. Varushka was looking at them and they were trying to read her blank eyes.

Varushka cleared her throat, forced a smile, and mumbled, "We are getting a divorce." Her eyes betrayed the sadness behind her smile. Arshiya, Aniket, and Kesha froze in their positions, stealing glances at each other. Nishav was sitting quietly under the blanket next to Varushka. The joyous aura vanished all of a sudden.

"Cheers guys! I am getting divorced, not committing suicide." Varushka raised her glass and everyone else followed her.

The clinking of glasses followed with a "Cheers!"

"It was definitely the worst joke of the evening," said Kesha, keeping her head on Varushka's lap.

"It was certainly *not* a joke!" Varushka confirmed. Everyone froze.

"But why? Who the hell gets a divorce within four months of marriage?" said Arshiya. "It takes some time to establish harmony with each other."

The Celebration

Ten months ago

It was four in the evening already. In the four years of engineering, all the lowbrows were socialising with all the highbrows, smiling unremittingly for the second and last time in their engineering life. The first time they got introduced to each other was four years back, during the fresher induction program.

However, this time it was the inaugural day of placements.

The inaugural day of placements at an engineering college is much like a hurricane. There is filth and chaos everywhere. In a day, dozens of companies come to the campus and fight for the best B.Tech Grad of the college.

Varushka had enough reason to be hopeful of an early placement. Her marks were outstanding. Her résumé was filled with academic achievements with an awesome list of extracurricular activities that she took part in. She took pride in the fact that when anyone considered her on the whole, she had quite enough reasons to anticipate an early signing off from the placement procedure.

Technesight Ltd. was a much sought after employer on her campus: a hefty salary, good brand and great exposure. They were known to hand over challenging work to new recruits as well.

When Varushka saw her name among the shortlisted candidates in the Technesight Ltd. list, she recalled the motivational video that she had seen on her mobile. She bucked herself up and sipped her fifth coffee for the day. She knew that she was overdoing the caffeine part, but she needed to maintain the energy level in her body and her voice. She knew it was always better to be energetic in a group discussion.

"Friends, let's now analyse it from this point of view..."

"In today's technological era…"

The same sentences were recapped in every group discussion. As usual, she cleared it.

Having seen the previous candidate for the interview coming out with a smile, Varushka took a cursory glance through her résumé. She had three minutes before the interview and she had to decide between another dose of caffeine or water to calm down her nerves. She checked her energy level and realized that she could do without one more cup of coffee. She opted for a glass of chilled water instead before going into the washroom.

She looked at the mirror and saw her immaculately ironed light blue shirt under the midnight blue blazer. She saw her brown eyes and checked the kohl. The kohl enhanced the spellbinding beauty of her eyes.

The good part was that she never had to apply any cosmetics on her face. Her bronze skin was naturally clean and even toned.

A boon, which along with her good height of five feet four inches and mesmerising eyes, made people's heads turn.

She came out of the washroom, joined her hands and said a short prayer.

After that, she stepped into the interview room.

▼

Two young men along with a senior man were sitting in the room, somberness written on their faces. Their faces softened upon seeing Varushka.

"Hi Varushka! Tell us something about yourself. Something that your résumé doesn't reveal about you."

Varushka took five seconds to recollect all the important points that she had mugged.

"Thank you, sir. My name is Varushka Jha. I am twenty-one years old and I'd describe myself as a person with a versatile skill-set, a lot of integrity and a willingness to go the extra mile to complete the challenges I take and learn something novel. I generally like to browse about the latest happenings in the programming world. The regular reading of these topics has led me to start learning up-and-coming languages like Python and Javascript through online tutorials.

"Personally, I am a person who believes in the simple joys of life. I love to paint landscapes in my free time."

"Interesting. But I don't think your painting skills are going to help our organisation."

She smiled. "I think painting is one of the most important skills I have. It's helped me develop higher levels of concentration and also taught me the importance of patience and perseverance in order to put the different colours delicately on the blank canvas. For me, a painting session would help with eloquence and relaxation after a challenging day at work."

"It is great to see a young girl like you being so thoughtful. How would you rate yourself as a leader?"

"I rate my leadership skills an 8 out of 10. There is much to learn, but I have always been a strong leader. I am somebody who believes that women are at par with men and should rub shoulders with them. So I would love to prove myself by taking up any challenging role."

"Are you sure you would be able to adapt to the challenging environment of the workplace? How flexible a person are you?"

"Sir, I am somebody with minimalist needs. I have been raised and molded in adapting to any new environment in no time. The challenge of coping with the academic rigour of NIT has also trained me adequately. I have always been highly adaptive and my diligence helps me pick up new stuff quickly.

"Since I am clear about my job role and I am mentally prepared to take up challenges, I feel I have the capacity to learn fast and apply my new knowledge. During my student life, I had to clear new papers and projects every semester and thoroughly enjoyed doing it. Similarly, I will enjoy picking up new technologies in my professional life as well."

That was an utter lie. When she needed the dress she had seen somewhere, she needed it at any cost. When she needed her cup of green tea, she needed her cup of green tea; to hell with flexibility. But such descriptions were never a hit with interviewing HRs.

"Have you ever run away after being assigned a very difficult task?'

"No sir. I am famous on the campus for finishing everything that I start. I would love to take up any challenge that Technesight throws at me."

Even bigger a lie! Her eyes shifted to her résumé in the interviewer's hand. Half of the projects on her résumé were unfinished projects. She had conveniently forgotten to mention the unfinished part in her résumé. She had this knack of finishing every project only up to the stage where she could mention it on her résumé and then quit.

"If you won a million dollar lottery, would you still work?"

"Yes, I would still work to build my career. No amount is comparable to my dreams. As far as the lottery money is concerned, I will buy a huge house for my parents."

"Do you have any questions?"

"No, sir."

She always believed in replying with a 'No sir' to that question. Asking questions could show doubt towards the recruiter. You might seem sharp, but recruiters never like questions.

"Great then, all I can say is that I hope you will like working with Technesight. You will be joining on the second of August."

This was more explicit than usual for a campus placement interview. Normally they say 'I hope you would like...' and stop. However, Varushka was given the joining date as well.

They shook hands. She exited with a broad smile.

▼

Officially, the final list came out at eight in the night. Varushka saw the list on the first day of the placement. By the time, half of her batch was already placed. She walked towards the café where Kesha, Nishav, Arshiya and Aniket were sitting with the whole batch. The happy boys and girls with jobs in their kitties were celebrating their success by pouring fizzy cold drinks on each other, smearing the cake on their faces.

Aniket and Kesha looked at Varushka and showed her the cake in their hands.

"Don't worry, not here. We will do it with chocolate and ketchup, but once we have reached Varushka's home," giggled Kesha.

Arshiya and Aniket had got placed in Zeal Infotech, while Nishav and Kesha had got placed in HW. Hers could have been the worst résumé in the history of HW. However, she had the impressive qualities to make up for her shortcomings.

"So, how are we celebrating?" Varushka asked Kesha.

"Why do you even ask such a stupid question?"

"You mean food and shopping, don't you?"

Kesha grinned. "I have one more plan to add to this. How about a trip to the northeast? Only we two. I am sure they are going to send us far from this place. Then we don't know when we both will get time to come here together.

"This will be the last time we will be spending our parent's money on travelling and shopping," she said.

Both of them screamed with excitement.

▼

Varushka could barely wait to tell her parents, but she somehow managed to make it home without bursting with happiness. She didn't want to do it over the phone.

Warm and giddy in exhilaration, Varushka climbed up the stairs, two steps at a time. Someone had left an open dustbin with stale leftover food in the corner, which made the whole staircase smell like rotten onions. Normally, that would have annoyed Varushka, but she just giggled it off. It took her a while to find the right key and insert it in the lock; her fingers were trembling with excitement.

"Yo. Are you drunk or something?" Rhea, Varushka's younger sister asked, appearing on the other side of the metal mesh door screen, while opening it for her.

"Kind of," Varushka giggled, walking in. "Well, no, not drunk. But I'm definitely in high spirits. I got selected, Rhea. I got the job."

"Whoa. That's awesome!" Rhea turned around immediately and called out, "Mom, Dad! Di got the job!"

Varushka followed Rhea inside. Her mom appeared with a tomato in her hand, and her dad also came running.

"What did you say?" they asked together.

"Di got the job!" Rhea said again.

"Which company? What package have they offered?" her dad asked excitedly.

"Di, you have really worked so hard all these years. It must feel like a dream turning into reality, eh?" Rhea said, picking up a sliced beetroot from the salad bowl on the dining table.

"Yep. I'm still quite amazed," Varushka replied.

"Quite reasonable," Rhea said looking around. "Where is Mom, though? I am hungry."

Just then they heard their mom talking enthusiastically on the phone "...yes, yes. Thank you. It's all god's grace. We were worried too, but she worked very hard..."

"Boasting to the relatives," her dad said, smiling.

"I will finish making dinner. What is she cooking?" Varushka said, going into the kitchen. She checked the pans on the stove.

"*Lauki ka kofta* and *dal tadka*. The *dal tadka* is done, kofta curry needs a few more minutes. Rhea, can you set the table? I will get started on the *rotis*."

When her mom was done calling and bragging to all the women in the neighbourhood and relatives with the news, she came back and hugged Varushka. They sat down and had dinner together, rejoicing her achievement. Varushka looked around the dinner table and felt ecstatic. Getting her parents to be proud of her was gratifying indeed.

▼

When Varushka woke up the next morning, she heard voices in the living room. She got dressed for college and went to the kitchen to get her breakfast, regretting it immediately. She would prefer skipping breakfast over talking to Manisha Maasi, her mother's cousin who refused to stop being a part of all their family affairs.

"Namaste, maasi," Varushka said, smiling sweetly. She didn't care, but her mother did, so pretentions needed to be kept up.

"Namaste beta, how are you? Congratulations on your placement!"

"I am doing good, and thank you!" Varushka served herself some *ghugni* and roasted *chura* from the pot on the stove.

"Your mother and I were just talking about how important education, a job and career are for a woman."

"Yeah?" Varushka sat down to eat, planning on gulping down her breakfast at top speed and getting the hell out of there as soon as possible.

"Yes. Boys nowadays are demanding not only simple educated girls, but prefer those who are working. See my Ranchi *wale* brother-in-law – six months back he brought a product manager bahu working in a Dubai firm. Everyone in the society still talks about them. As the girl held such a big post, they reduced their dowry demand from thirty-five lakhs to twenty-five lakhs."

"Ten l-a-k-h-s less!" Varushka's mother dropped her jaw.

"That is why I am saying that there will be even better proposals for Varushka. Our Varushka has studied engineering from NIT and has got a job in such an internationally reputed company, and such a high salary. If you say, should I talk to my sister-in-law? Her brother's son has completed his MBA from a business college in London and now he is working for a multinational company in Hyderabad. If I will push this, they might close the deal within twenty lakhs only!"

Varushka concentrated on swallowing her food without choking.

"Maasi, so what you mean to say is your brother-in-law brought a bahu home and that bahu's family bought a groom? Am I correct?"

Varushka's mother and Manisha Maasi looked at each other, baffled.

"Chuck it!"

"Didn't your brother-in-law's bahu leave her job as per the order of your brother-in-law?" Varushka egged them on.

"Ah, nothing like that, it was her own wish. Family's responsibilities had increased and family is always the priority for a woman. Isn't it, Di?" Manisha Maasi said, beaming.

Varushka contemplated telling them that the bahu they were speaking about was a school friend's elder sister, but decided she was above that.

She said bye to her mom and left.

A First Meeting

F ew weeks passed in celebration before a new chapter started in their lives. Most of her friends had gone back to their hometowns. Kesha had come over to Varushka's place to hang out that day.

"Any word from Technesight?" Kesha asked, as she entered Varushka's house.

"Received a mail in the morning."

"…and what does it say?"

"I have three months to finish my shopping, complete café and restaurant hopping in Patna and to create beautiful memories with my loved ones here before signing the contract of the new chapter of my life. My professional life!" Varushka said, proudly hugging Kesha.

"But where is the location? I am joining on the 2nd of August in Gurgaon."

"Really? Me too! Now we will rock in Gurgaon together! And when we will miss home and home food, we'll hop over to Nishav's home. Stuffed parathe made by Aunty with scrumptious chutneys and delicious lassi… ummm."

"Yayyy!" both the girls chattered, running towards Varushka's room.

▼

Varushka lay down in her bed at night, waiting to fall asleep. Her mind oscillated between wonderful thoughts of fulfilling her dreams of travelling to all the destinations on her bucket list, sending her parents on a trip, buying a solitaire ring for her mother and so on. Her mom came to her room and switched on the light.

She came and sat next to Varushka on the bed.

"They're coming home tomorrow for evening tea."

Varushka looked at her in a dilemma.

"Mom, I don't… oh mom, why are you so serious about my marriage? I have just received the offer letter and haven't even joined. Moreover, my final exams aren't over yet."

Taking a pause. "Don't worry, I don't have a boyfriend that I will elope with. I will marry the one you and Dad will choose. Why the hurry, mom? I need some time, and you too, take some time…"

"Time? Some more time? You people think I always speak rubbish. How will you understand the feeling of a mother? How big the responsibility of a daughter's marriage is?"

"And was it not your dream since I was born that I get a good education, get a good job and be a self-dependent woman? You always said that you wanted me to earn my own money, have my identity and dignity. When I am about to fulfil your dreams, winning over all the milestones, why do you want to fetter my steps to my destination at the last moment?"

"Did I ever neglect your needs? Clothes, sports, food, education, entertainment, and hobbies – whatever you've asked for, we've tried our best to give it to you. Can't you do me a small favour for my happiness?"

It was the *Bhrahmastra* – the master weapon that is thrown by mothers to end the discussion in their favour.

Varushka picked a cushion and hit her own face hard.

"Let me sleep if it does not imply disrupting your happiness."

"Thank you so much, darling. I know you would never disappoint your mother. Sleep well!" Varushka's mother jumped up with joy.

After her mother left, Varushka shrugged and slid back into bed. She fell asleep to enter the world of her dream life – working with a multinational company, exploring the world, sending her parents on an exotic holiday and shopping to her heart's content.

▼

The distinctive and intense aroma of asafoetida woke Varushka up. She sneezed once, and then again before she got up and checked the time on her phone. 7:30 a.m. She was surprised with the noise coming from outside her room. It was an unusual Sunday morning with everyone very much up and about so early.

She put her phone aside and got up. She wrapped her hair in a high bun, washed her face, freshened up and went out of her room.

Generally, on Sunday, Varushka's family had brunch at 11 a.m. However, today breakfast was ready at 7:30 a.m. Varushka was still wondering what was special as either it was a special occasion or her mom was very happy. She had made *dalpudi* and *kheer* and that too, for breakfast.

"Good morning," Mom said, looking pointedly at Varushka's hair and night suit. Varushka followed her gaze, puzzled.

"You are not ready? What have you decided?"

"…as if you have left me with a choice," Varushka mumbled.

"What?"

"Mom! Again!"

"You only said that you need some time. I thought nine hours of the long night were enough."

"What? You want me to think the whole night instead of sleeping? Phew."

"Do you need more time?" her mother asked innocently as if everything was normal. "Would five hours be enough?"

Varushka saw her face and then turned to her father. She wanted to say something but he put his hand on hers, indicating her to be quiet. Then there was the masterstroke used by Indian parents to convince their children.

"If your mother is insisting so much, meet the boy once. She is asking only to meet the boy, not to marry. Chill! We'll think about the other stuff later," Dad smiled at his witty speech.

"Oh yeah! You are great, Dad," Varushka smiled back.

"Later you can say that you didn't find the boy suitable. No one would compel you to say 'yes'. For now, close this matter," Dad whispered this time.

"Okay Mom, you can tell Manisha Maasi that I am ready for this meeting. But not at our home."

Varushka wanted to keep things discreet.

Though no one imposes it, they opt for other ways of emotional wile and blackmailing, Varushka thought.

▼

Varushka wore a teal crepe saree with a sleeveless blouse. The black eyeliner around her eyes and maroon lipstick enhanced her wheatish warm complexion.

Varushka's mom didn't want to be late, so she reached half an hour before the fixed time. Manisha Maasi was already there. She seemed even more excited.

"I have spoken to the manager here and instructed them properly. They will not leave a single aspect to impress the boy's family."

Varushka was amused at Manisha Maasi's words as her mother took a deep breath of satisfaction.

"Dad, I thought we came here to meet the boy and his family for my wedding, but here Mom and Manisha Maasi are cooking up something else. They seem to have come for a business deal."

▼

At 5 p.m. two women and two older men entered the café together. A man in his late twenties followed them. The young man was six feet tall with a lean physique and was dressed in a crisp light grey shirt with tapered charcoal trousers. He wore a drooping, bristly moustache with a shiny goatee. His champagne brown eyes flickered with curiosity over a genial smile that annoyed Varushka.

"Ugh… I am already hating his moustache and his smile. God, how long would I have to tolerate him?" she whispered to herself.

Manisha Maasi with Varushka's parents welcomed them.

They settled down.

"She is my better half. Here is my elder son Aadarsh – a cardiologist, and his wife Madhu, MBA Finance topper from Jain University, Bangalore. He is Sarthak, my son – your could-be son-in-law." While the others simply smiled at this lame joke, Sarthak's father thought he sounded cool.

Now it was Varushka's father's turn to prove himself equally cool.

Varushka was nervous, but then she remembered, she had nothing to lose.' She was prepared to go with an open mind and enjoy the conversation she was going to have with these new people. That's what was playing in Varushka's mind when she sat down after the initial awkward introductions.

Manisha Maasi had already instructed the café manager about what had to be served and when. They got some coffee with some snacks, and then the Q & A round started. Sarthak was sitting across Varushka, while his mother decided to bombard her with questions she wanted to ask her potential bahu.

Then, she started to cross-check all the glorious statements made so excitedly in the bio-data forwarded by Varushka's parents though Manisha Maasi.

"You like cooking, you have mentioned. What do you enjoy cooking the most?"

"You have done some modelling before, do you plan to continue that?" Phew! While the father and son were just smiling and nodding their heads, Varushka's parents were praying. Varushka was almost gloating about all her victories in her life. As time passed, both the families became calm and comfortable.

Time was passing by quickly. After about an hour, Varushka noticed she hadn't got any alone time with Sarthak. The person inside of her wanted to really see the possibility of finding 'the one' in case things worked out.

She wanted this arranged-date to break the conventional stereotype about an arranged wedding meeting. At least she would have some interesting tales to share! Moreover, she was interested in exploring all the possible reasons to say no to marry this nerd.

Varushka's father read her eyes. "If it's alright, can Varushka and Sarthak talk alone for a bit, to know each other?" he said. At first, Sarthak's family was startled, obviously.

"Of course! We are modern Biharis," Sarthak's father gave his approval. "Sarthak, Varushka and you go and talk."

Sarthak and Varushka went away to a table close by and started chatting about life. Her throat was bad so she decided to order some fancy smoked tea and Sarthak got himself some black coffee.

"Actually, I don't know what to ask you. This is the first time I am meeting anybody like this." Sarthak tried to begin the conversation.

"Yeah, same here. I am also meeting a guy for the first time for a marriage, but I don't mind asking the questions," Varushka smiled, wickedly.

True, for Varushka, it wasn't too tough to start a conversation, now that she had passed the test in front of his parents.

"Tell me about your family?" she began with the general round.

"My dad is a retired Air Force pilot and now successfully running his business in Hyderabad. My dad had introduced my elder brother and sister-in-law when we came in. Bro is a cardiaologist. They got married six months back. I guess, you must have read everything about me in my biodata," Sarthak replied.

"Yeah. Everything that was written, but I am sure there must be many more, untold-unseen stories."

"You are really smart."

"That is true." She smiled. "Anyway, you did not tell me about Madhu bhabhi. Where does she work?"

"She is not working."

"…helping out your Dad in his business?"

Sarthak laughed. "She is helping out Mom. Dad is capable to handle it all alone and my bro is helping him by taking care of our family."

"Oh I see…" Though Varushka wanted to ask that if she had wanted to work in the kitchen, why did she study Finance and scored high in her subjects, but she bit her lip. She was not here for a debate with him. She decided to enjoy the evening lightly, considering it a break from her monotonous holidays.

They spoke for a while about likes and dislikes, college life, and then they came to the question about their life skills and hobbies.

"So how do you tackle stress or are you busy with something?" Sarthak asked.

"I shop," the chatterbox Varushka replied immediately.

"Shopping? How can shopping be a stress buster? Anyway, I was asking you about your hobbies or something you are very much interested in."

"That's what I am saying. I just love shopping, whether I am very happy or sad. I go shopping, try stuff, window shop while chatting with my friends or family. It is so much fun, you know."

"I see... I pity your future husband. All his hard earned money will be spent shopping, I guess!" Sarthak chuckled.

"Aah... nothing to worry about. I always shop with my own money. I anyway will earn enough for my expenses and very soon will be capable of taking care of even my husband's expenses," Varushka smiled sarcastically.

"Don't you sound too feminist?" Sarthak laughed.

"Really? But isn't spending your hard-earned money something normal?"

"I was just kidding about the money part, but you were offended, I guess."

"Not at all, even I was kidding."

"What's the problem with girls these days? Why are you always ready for war, wearing your women empowerment crown?"

"I didn't say anything like that. Before seeing myself as a girl and you as a man, I see us as human beings. That's it! But I don't understand why you guys find it so offensive when a girl talks about money or career. If you can't respect the dreams, dignity, desires of a human being of all genders..."

He butted in angrily, "I can give you as much money as you need to shop, and keep your money for your other enjoyments. You won't even need to work for money."

"Now this sounds stereotypical..." Varushka smiled.

"What do you mean?"

"Chuck it!" Varushka dismissed it casually.

"...And one more thing, you should behave well with your owners. The one who has come to buy you from your dad. Someone being sold does not have the right to raise her voice like this."

There was no point in continuing the discussion. A big scene had already been created in the café. Varushka's dad paid the bill and everyone left.

▼

"What did you do? How good that family was!" Varushka's mom shouted as she sat in their white Fiat car. Her dad was trying to concentrate on driving and reaching home safely.

"You would have lived like a queen there. They are so rich!" Manisha Maasi was adding fuel to the fire.

"Like our queens Kritika Maasi and Sharda Bua? They don't even have the right to meet their siblings, friends, without taking permission from their husbands? The ones who keep complaining about their life and the ones who wish they could have been working now..."

"That's what your education teaches you! To talk to your parents in such a way..."

"Oh Mom… now don't start saying women are born to keep crying about their fate and keep blaming them for being born, as my education doesn't allow me to do that."

At First Sight

Two weeks later, Varushka returned home after her last exam. Her parents were enjoying their evening tea with Manisha Maasi.

"Varushka was right that day. Only by portraying yourself as modern won't make you modern if you can't take a girl's career and professional passion positively."

Varushka was about to choke while sipping her coffee. She stared at Manisha Maasi, wondering what had made her change her mind in two weeks. She was the one accusing her of letting go of a superb *rishta*!

"What are you saying?" Varushka's mother questioned in surprise.

Varushka and her dad got ready to witness some drama.

"…And what made you think so finally?" her dad asked.

"Mitash."

"Mitash?" everyone else repeated.

"My sister-in-law who lives in Ranchi… her husband's cousin Rinki has bought a new house in Patna. They threw a housewarming party last Friday. Rinki is close to me, so she made me stay at their home for the night. Her son had also come down. He lives in Amsterdam and is working with a big company at a big-big position, earning crores in a year."

"Hmm..." Varushka was waiting for the secret to be revealed.

"We were simply talking about marriages nowadays. Rinki is also looking for a suitable bride for her son. So as we were chatting, I narrated the Sarthak incident, that how rude and orthodox a few people are, even when they project themselves as modern.

"Then Mitash also joined our conversation. He is very progressive and believes that women need to get higher education, a job and freedom to fulfil their dreams. Listening to the story, he remembered the incident and place. Coincidentally, he was at the café that day. He saw what happened and was praising the courage and decision of the girl – our talented Varushka."

"But who is Mitash?" Finally, Varushka's mother lost her patience and enquired.

"That's what I am explaining na. Mitash is Rinki's only son. The main thing is that they were very impressed with Varushka. And now Mitash wants to marry her."

Then looking at Varushka, she added with a smile, "If she agrees, of course!"

Varushka's mother's jaw dropped. "Really?" Her dad looked at her.

"God! Not again. I don't understand why you are all in such a hurry to get me married!" Varushka screamed and went off to her room, giving Manisha Maasi enough space and time to brag about her sister-in-law and nephew, and to convince Varushka's parents to accept Rinki's proposal.

"Rarely does it happen that a groom's side sends a proposal. Moreover, it could be a great opportunity to bargain on the dowry," Manisha Maasi was trying to press the right nerve. "Seeing the profile of the family's property and the boy's education, job and salary, they would easily get a minimum of fifty lakhs from anywhere else. However, they give more value to a person's virtues."

"They have liked Varushka so much, and it seems everyone earns in crores. So they cannot even ask for dowry, *hai na?*"

"You know our society. If the groom's side does not ask for dowry or less dowry, people think something is wrong with the boy. Society enjoys spreading such rumours," she giggled. "But don't worry. I will do something that'll work out well. I know you both will manage the little add-ons. Afterall, whatever is yours belongs to both your daughters na. Soon they will be settled happily ever after."

"But how are we to convince Varushka? After the last incident, she won't even agree to meet anyone!"

"Don't worry, di. This time it is different. Mitash lives in a foreign place, and he wants to talk to Varushka first, before the families meet."

"But how?"

Manisha Maasi interrupted, "Leave the how and when to me. He is going to find a way, but first, you say yes. I have already forwarded Varushka's biodata."

"If this wedding takes place, I'll gift you a designer saree to wear at the wedding, of your choice…"

▼

Seeing kheer on the table, Varushka understood that Manisha Maasi had succeeded in casting a spell on her mother. Her mother made her special kheer only when she was extremely happy.

To her surprise, no one discussed Rinki, Mitash or the wedding proposal at all. Varushka decided it was better to remain silent and not to take the risk of starting such a topic.

▼

Before sleeping, Varushka was checking out the photos that someone had shot of her college friends, on the last day of the college. Someone had posted them on Facebook and tagged Varushka. While she was looking at the photos, she noticed a new friend request. A message notification popped up.

Hi,

I'm Mitash.

I hope you have come to know about me through Manisha aunty, and about the wedding proposal as well.

I want to marry a girl with a dream and passion to fulfil it. Someone who will take a stand for her rights and her own life. I would like a girl who loves herself and takes her own decisions and has a professional goal. When I saw you and heard your conversation followed by the argument with that guy, I really wished to meet you once if I could. And luckily, god gave me a chance.

I don't know whether you are going to accept this proposal or not. If yes, I don't want us to begin in that typical way. So I want to meet you and discuss and decide how to proceed before our families arrange the formal meeting.

Will be waiting for your reply.

"My goodness. Manisha Maasi was serious!" Varushka whispered to herself.

She clicked on the friend request. It was Mitash. She was confused whether she should accept or decline the request, or simply ignore it. As she was thinking about that, she knew was no longer in a position to ignore it.

She opened his profile and scrolled for another hour viewing his photos, activities, comments in his posts – everything that she could see without accepting the request.

"Seems cool," Varushka said to herself while accepting the friend request finally. "But strangely, why didn't Mom utter a single word about this at the dinner table?"

There was something special about Mitash, so much so that she could not simply ignore him. She wrote a message in reply.

Hi Mitash,

Thanks for writing, and your attitude towards girls really impressed me.

I am not sure about the marriage meeting as yet. The last time I only went because of the pressure my parents put on me. That compelled me to meet that guy, unwillingly.

However, I feel, there is nothing wrong in meeting over a cup of coffee.

Regards,

Varushka

The very next minute, her mobile flashed with the arrival of a new Facebook message.

Mitash: Thanks for accepting the request, friendship and to meet.
Are you free tomorrow?

Varushka: What time?

Mitash: You say...

Varushka: Any time after 1 p.m. as I have some work in the morning.

Mitash: Sure. Any place in mind?

Varushka: Would be great if you choose one.

Mitash: 👍

After ten minutes, there was a new message from Mitash.

The Dining Room at 1:30 p.m. Now sleep soon, so that you get up early tomorrow and finish all your work before we meet :)
Send me your number, in case we need to call.

She replied with a smiley and a goodnight sticker along with her number.

▼

It was eight in the morning and Varushka was still in bed when her phone rang.

"Hello!" she said in a sleepy voice.

"Good morning, sunshine," said a sweet voice from the other end.

"Good morning! May I know who's calling?"

"This is Mitash. I am hoping our plan for lunch is still on."

Hearing the name Mitash, Varushka was all awake. She quickly recalled the previous night's chat.

"Lunch or coffee?"

"The weather outside is really amazing today. Let's have lunch at 2 o'clock and then coffee as well. Oh, and save my number!"

"No problem. I will be there on time."

Though she had said yes, Varushka wasn't able to decide whether to go or not.

▼

It was already 1:30 p.m. and Varushka hadn't decided what she would wear. The fluttering in her heart refused to die down. She realized that she had never dressed up this way for anyone. She applied the eyeliner and mascara that she used only for special occasions. Then, she used a sheer magenta lip gloss that made her lips look fuller. She selected one of the new outfits that she had bought for her last college party.

'Dressed to kill,' she thought, as she glanced at herself in the mirror, feeling childishly pleased. She had worn a blue dress with a delicate lace border and a pair of Catwalk turquoise and cream heels.

As she started her Fiat, there was a text from Mitash.

Hurry, I am waiting at The Dining Room.

Driving. See you in 15 minutes, she texted back.

▼

When she finally saw him, he was bent over his smartphone, both legs stretched out. A half-finished Setting Sun Mocktail was on the table as he was completely engrossed with whatever he was doing. He looked as handsome as he did in the photos. Varushka could see that he looked after his body too. He was toned and fit, his half-sleeved black T-shirt showing off muscular arms which must have pumped iron for hours in a gym. His hair was stylishly cut. Black full rimmed glasses were making his face look even more appealing.

Varushka stood and stared at him for a few seconds, taking in every detail about him. Then she walked up to his table and said, "Hi."

Mitash looked up and his gaze met her eye. She couldn't look away; she immediately felt locked in. The look of startled surprise changed into slow recognition and then his eyes lit up in pure joy as a million-watt smile flashed across his face.

"God, you're even more beautiful than your pictures," he said.

"Do you ever say anything with such seriousness?" she sighed, trying to cover her burning blush.

"Being serious is not important. I believe in being truthful, and more so, a bit practical."

"Aha… impressive!" she said smiling.

Mitash pulled out the chair for her.

"What would you like to have?" Mitash asked rotating the menu card towards her.

"I would like to have Pasta Penne Alfredo in white sauce."

"Aah… what a fool I am! I got a gift for you. Seeing you, I forgot everything." Mitash smiled as he bent to open a paper bag next to him.

"And here is a small gift for you," Mitash offered a bunch of blue and white orchids and a small box wrapped with red handmade paper.

"It's so beautiful!" her eyes shone with gratitude and amazement.

"It has to be; it is in the hands of a gorgeous lady."

Varushka couldn't conceal her blush.

"Mitash, there was really no need for this. But thanks a lot. Can I open it?" Varushka said pointing to the tiny box.

"Sure… but after lunch. I am damn hungry."

"I am missing the wine with the pasta," Mitash said as he tasted the first bite with a mischievous grin.

"Ssshh… don't even say that. Nowadays it is considered illegal even imagining such things here," Varushka said and both of them burst into laughter together.

"I learnt that you completed your B.Tech and also got a job offer from a reputed company. When are you going to join them?"

"Yep, my training is going to start next month," she said proudly.

"It is really impressive to see girls from Bihar so serious and passionate about their careers."

"I think they were in the past as well. Unfortunately, for most of the families, marriage is priority."

"Umm, I agree. But what if you get both together?"

"I didn't get you."

"First tell me, why don't you want to get married?"

"I don't want to get married *now*. I haven't even started my career as yet and I have seen most girls are asked to either not work or put in the papers soon after their marriage. However, the guy's family wants their bahu to be higly educated and professionally qualified. I seriously don't understand their point."

"Calm down, girl! I agree with you, but not everyone is like that. I want to marry a girl who has a dream and a passion for her career. Someone who would be my best friend and with whom I can discuss my career, not just family issues. By the way, do you like travelling?"

"Travelling! It's my dream to travel around the world."

"Which places have you seen?"

"I have been to Rajasthan, Gujarat, Delhi, Kashmir, Sikkim, Meghalaya, Arunachal Pradesh and a few others in the east, but have never been to the west or southern India. I am sure you must have gone to many places in Europe and America."

"Great! True, I have travelled to a lot of countries and also in our country. I love solo travelling."

"Solo travelling? It is one of my biggest dreams, you know!" her eyes sparkled as she said with all her excitement. "I want to save a big amount of my salary to travel all around the globe."

"I hope it comes true!" he replied with a wider dazzling smile.

"I have never been allowed to travel alone. It has always been with friends and not beyond the boundary of Bihar." Her face saddened. "My college friends wanted to go to Goa or Bhutan on a group trip before we all part. However, we ended up settling for a small local picnic."

"Where here?"

"Nalanda!"

"Wow. I had been there when I was a kid. I always wished to go again, but it never happened."

"There is nothing wow compared to a trip to Goa."

"For me, when it is a group, company matters, not the place. When it comes to a solo trip, the place matters."

"Hmm… you didn't tell me anything about yourself."

"I was assuming you would have checked my social media profiles."

"Haha… I learnt about your tastes, likes and dislikes, your fun-filled life to some extent through your Facebook, Twitter and Instagram accounts. Your LinkedIn profile screams a lot about your academic and professional achievements. There is a lot more we never share on any of these portals. So what about you? Your dreams and everything that you would want to tell me!"

Mitash looked at her with a boyishly amused look on his face.

"Okay, tell me when did you come back from Amsterdam and when are you going back?"

"One week is already over and I have forty-five days to go. The fact is Mom and Dad desperately want me to get married so that they can have a daughter-in-law who can keep a tab on me, regularly updating them about my pranks in Amsterdam. They are looking for a girl and want me to either get married or at least get engaged before I go back."

"Gosh! Does that really happen? I used to think it was just in Bollywood scripts that an NRI comes to India, sees a girl, gets married in a week or two and then goes back with or without the wife, sometimes," she said with a chuckle.

"Being a well-travelled person, collecting so many experiences, how did you get ready to marry someone just by looking at her beauty and then fixing a deal of a lifetime? Isn't it like procuring furniture or accessories? A ten minute-talk or even an hour-long conversation won't help in knowing a person," she added.

"But to know a person, don't you think even a whole life is too short many times? More than knowing, understanding the other person is more important. Self-belief that you are capable enough to make things right if they go wrong sometimes helps. We can't know a person completely, although we know ourselves. Talking and spending some time with the other person can help understand whether we will be able to adjust with their life or if the other person is meant to share ours," he replied.

"Oh my goodness! What a philosophical explanation! I am sure you must have had many girlfriends who have enlightened you," she laughed teasingly.

"I have had many girls as friends, but I was never in a serious relationship with any girl as I was focused on building my career," he replied confidently and smiled.

"I can trust your eyes." She winked, being flirtatious.

"Varushka, after seeing you that day at the café and now talking to you, I am sure that we'll make a perfect couple."

"But Mitash, I don't want to get married and end my dreams. So when you said you support my belief, then how...."

Varushka was cut short by Mitash.

"Varushka, you want a career... now what if I promise you to make even a better career for you. Even better than what you got as an offer, I can get you one in..."

Varushka interrupted, "But why? Why do you want to marry me when you can get many other girls, maybe even better than me?"

"I am not someone who leaves the best opportunity in front and moves on in search of a hopeful better or second best. Your charm, your aura and attitude is something that could better understand me and would make an ideal better half for me. Family, emotions, relationships do matter for me, but my dreams and career are also important. A person like you can understand all these as you have the same spirit and conviction about life."

"So you mean to say we get into a deal, Mitash – making my own identity and career is of course my dream. It is also not a fact that I don't have any expectations regarding marriage. I would prefer to fall in love and get married to that person. Please don't have the perception that a career oriented girl will sacrifice her personal and love life for her profession. I will wait until I find someone to balance it."

Mitash looking at her smiling, "What if your parents fix your wedding with someone else? So for your career, would you run away on your wedding day like it happened in *Badrinath ki Dulhania* or *Shaadi Mein Zaroor Aana*?"

A shocked Varushka burst out laughing and Mitash joined her.

Their tête-à-tête began formally, but in no time, it had become quite relaxed and casual. They talked for more than an hour. They noticed their lunch was over long back and the waiter was there again to ask if they wanted anything else.

"Hot chocolate?" Mitash said and looked at Varushka. He seemed to want to spend some more time with her, she thought.

"I love it!"

"By the time it arrives, would you like to unwrap your gift?"

Varushka started unwrapping the beautiful packet.

She skipped a heartbeat when she opened the box. A dazzling cushion cut solitaire diamond was set in platinum with petals of a red rose over it.

Everything seemed like a dream – a fairy tale or romantic movie script. Varushka couldn't utter a word, unable to understand what was happening and how to respond.

Shocked and confused, Varushka said, "Mitash, I can't take this."

"But why?"

"I can't take such a costly gift from someone I barely know. Don't you think it's too filmy and dramatic gifting someone such a special and expensive gift in a first meeting?"

"When I saw this ring once at a shop, I loved it so much that I bought it and decided to gift it to one who would touch my heart and become my better half. Varushka, you touched my heart the first day I saw you."

"Even then, I can't accept this ring, Mitash. Plus, I haven't said anything about marriage. Moreover, our parents haven't talked regarding this. But I accept the flowers and thanks for that."

"Okay, do this for me, keep it with you and return it when you make your final decision of not marrying me. Until then, please, as a favour, keep it with you."

"Sorry, Mitash. I can't. Keep it with you. If my final decision ever turns to yes, then you can give it to me again. Until then, please. And one more thing, we don't ever decide who we fall in love with. It eventually happens. I want to build my career first and when I'm financially stable, maybe I will get married too."

"Varushka, do you really think your family will accept this? Even if you say 'no' to me, they will find someone else. I guess, dating will consume all your energy. So Varushka, this proposal of mine is an ideal situation for both of us who are under the pressure of our parents forcing us to marry. Let's start our relationship as very good friends and simultaneously in time develop our career goals."

Varushka was feeling the warmth of the rushing blood in her veins. She took deep breaths to calm herself down.

"So, is this a kind of a deal, a proposition?"

"Whatever makes you comfortable."

"I still need time to think."

▼

That night, lying in her bed, Varushka went over the conversation with Mitash again and again. She wondered,

'Why have Mom and Dad not uttered a single word about this? Are they scared after the last times meeting with Sarthak and his family which I had messed up so badly? Why am I even thinking about all this when I am clear about my goals in life? First job, solo trip abroad and then getting married.'

Varushka Agrees

The smell of pepper and the devil's dung woke Varushka. She sneezed, and then again. She checked the time on her phone. 10.30 a.m. She was surprised that her mother hadn't woken her up. Usually, by this time, she would've yelled at her to get up or would've sent Rhea up.

'What's wrong?' she wondered. 'Why is mom using so much asafoetida in the morning?''

She sneezed again before stepping out of her room. There was chaos at home. Dad, Mom, Rhea were running helter skelter. Varushka saw a few extra heads in the house.

"Rheaaa... Rheaaa!" bellowed Varushka, going back to her bedroom.

Rhea came running in. "Di, coming. What happened? You woke up?"

"Nothing's happened to me. But, what's happening outside? Breakfast is already over and Mom never starts making lunch before 1 p.m. Why are these spicy aromas floating in the air at this time? By the way, who are those women? And why has no one come to wake me up until now?" Varushka bombarded Rhea with a volley of questions.

"Dad said that you slept late last night and instructed us to let you sleep... that's why." Confused with all the different questions, Rhea managed to answer the last one that she had heard properly.

"Hmmm… and what's happening at home?"

"What, di?"

"Gosh! I better ask Mom and Dad about it," said Varushka gruffly.

Varushka rushed to the kitchen. Her mom was busy stirring some curry. The maid was assisting her and was chopping some herbs.

"Shraddha Bua, youuuu!" Varushka suddenly screamed as she spied her aunt and embraced her tightly, "What a surprise! So, all this is happening for your welcome."

Shraddha Bua was one of Varushka's few favourite relatives. She was a lecturer in an engineering college and Varushka would often seek her guidance for her career, and sometimes for her personal life as well.

"You know na that your father and I were in the same college. One of our college friends has come to Patna after many years. Last week we met at a function. He wanted to meet Bhaiya too. Today he is coming with his family for lunch."

"Hmmm," Varushka nodded.

Varushka went to tidy her room and get ready to welcome the guests as everybody else was doing. Rhea had already cleaned up her room so she came to assist her sister.

Everyone in the family except Varushka was excited. Rather she was curious to know who the special guests were, for whom the whole family was so worked up.

Well, her wait was over when the doorbell rang at 12:30 p.m.
An elderly couple entered the house with a pretty girl close to
the ages of Varushka and Rhea. Introductions were soon over
and pleasantries exchanged.

Everyone was in a gala mood, including Varushka.
Mr Vikas Jha and Mrs Rinki Jha were quite a cool couple, unlike
other visitors. Their daughter Shrini was really sweet. Varushka
was enjoying their company and was happily engrossed in
conversation with them which was all related to youngsters'
education, career, dreams, trips and many such topics. For
a pleasant change, Mr and Mrs Jha didn't ask Varushka about
marriage – the question she hated. She found out that Shrini
was studying psychology in Bangalore and had an elder brother
as well who was stuck in an urgent meeting.

The gala-lunch was soon over. Varushka merrily let her mom
give Shrini a new dress which Varushka had bought recently as
a token of love. Mr and Mrs Jha had also brought gifts for Rhea
and Varushka.

▼

"So, Varushka," Mom said, "as I was saying..."

Varushka, Shraddha Bua and her mom were in the kitchen.

"You've said that five times. Do you actually have something
to say?" Varushka asked as she poured the tea into the cups.

"Shrini and her parents are so cool, no?" Finally, Mom
completed her sentence.

"Hmm," she replied. She passed Sharaddha bua a cup of tea.

"They want their only son to marry you. Mitash!"

"*What!*" a shocked Varushka spilled the tea on the kitchen
slab. "What do you mean?"

Mom and Shraddha Bua exchanged a silent glance.

"I am asking something. What are you two up to?" Varushka yelled.

"The Jhas are the same people about whom your Manisha Maasi was telling us," Mom said.

"Anyway you met their son, Mitash, yesterday," Shradda Bua quickly added.

"Buaa... you too!" Varushka steadied her head trying to understand the conspiracy.

"Oh, god! So this was all planned by you guys. Do you think there is a Bollywood shoot going on here?"

"Chill, beta. We thought you would get angry if we told you about Mitash's wedding proposal before. So we thought you could meet Mitash and his family and after that, you could decide," Shraddha Bua said.

"But who has liked that boy yet?" Varushka asked.

"Varushka, isn't it true that you liked them? You'd wish for a family like them to be your in-laws! They are career oriented like you always wanted and this could drive your goals and marriage as well. Think with a calm mind, dear."

"Sometimes think about your parents as well. We never stopped you from doing anything. We are your mom and dad, not the enemy that we will do something to harm you. You have a younger sister too. What will be the impact on Rhea if you won't listen to us?" Mom said and started sobbing, turning to Shraddha Bua. "Why don't these children understand us?"

"Mom, Bua, I've struggled so hard for all these years, and especially the last four years to get a good job. Now when it is in my hand, you all want me to drop it. Everyone dreams of this and right now it is in my hand. Marriage can happen even a few years later. I promise to marry as per your wish. First, let me fulfil my few dreams... actually they were our dreams na, Mom?"

"But we are offering you even better than that – a secured life."

"Do you give any guarantee for this so-called better and secured life? If yes, then I will marry him. If not, then you have to let me go."

"We assure you, cent per cent!" Mom did not take even a single second to think before she replied.

▼

The ring is waiting to get slipped on to your finger...

A message from Mitash flashed on her mobile screen.

Holding her joining letter in her hand, curling over the bed, Varushka was thinking whether she was really hurting her parents a lot? Were her aspirations for her dreams and dignity stupid thoughts? Was she really doing something wrong?

The whole night she dwelt upon the pros and cons of accepting this proposal and 'what if!' of not accepting the proposal.

On one side were her dreams, career and her life planning. The other side was her mother and father's society, *izzat, and the typical 'log kya kahenge'.*

▼

Not every wedding happens because the couple is in love. Some weddings are arranged marriages, while others are for 'the greater good'!

Next morning, torn pieces of her joining letter were scattered on the floor. Varushka's final decision was made.

The Marriage

Happiness floated like rose petals in the air.

Varushka wore a silver embroidered brocade lehenga. Her high prom-bun with its loose curls playing around her cheeks made her look like a doll. Her face had light makeup, and she looked prettier than ever. Her eyes looked deep, due to the kohl around it with dark smoky eyeshadow.

Her eyes met with those of Mitash, who was dressed in a turquoise kurta and off-white silk dhoti. Under the soft light of the chandeliers, his eyes shone. They were brown like hers. Maybe a shade or two darker. They were intense, and she found herself unable to break contact. He gave a little smile, enquiring about how he looked.

She nodded. Yes, he looked more handsome than he ever had. Even she was surprised as she was trying to see her life partner in him now.

The prayers continued for another hour. Aromatic smoke filled the room. The priests kept adding wood and spoonfuls of ghee to the fire. Varushka and Mitash exchanged glances and smiled several times. Was it really happening? Was she finally getting married, leaving her dream job offer? Adding her dreams to the fire and starting a new life.

Yes, she was getting socially and officially engaged with someone. She would be married to him soon. She was not leaving her dream behind. Instead, she had combined her dreams with her parents' dream.

It was not that she had never dreamt of getting married. She did. Although, the sequence of her life realm and planning were a bit different. Growing up watching Bollywood movies, she had thought she would find her 'dream prince' during one of her international solo trips and she would fall in love with him and eventually end up marrying him.

Mitash was on his knees before Varushka. The bride and groom's parents were on the stage surrounded by the applauding clan.

"As I place this ring on your finger, I commit my heart and soul to you forever," he said.

"This ring has no beginning nor end. I place it on your finger as the continuation of true love. I give you all that I am and ever hope to be," she replied as she slipped the engagement band on his finger, connecting herself to his heart.

She remembered the movies about love at first sight, meeting someone through friends and falling in love, office love stories and so many other such stories. Then she remembered one of the most beautiful love stories she knew ever – her mom and dad's love story. Theirs was an arranged marriage. Yet they still shared love which anyone could feel and sense as if they were newly-wed lovebirds. There was an aura of romance and charm when she saw them together.

That day she felt different emotions inside her. Everything seemed to be different. She felt her inner self was not the same that day. It was the beginning of a new chapter in her life.

A Day of Romance

One function was over. Many more were lined up.

At the suggestion of Manisha Maasi and Rhea, Varushka's mom agreed to plan a pre-wedding shoot for Varushka and Mitash so that they get some time to spend together and be comfortable. It was a kind of compensation in exchange for the children agreeing to an arranged marriage. A perfect occasion to step back from the exhaustive planning and have a day that was all about Varushka and Mitash.

Rhea had booked Meow-Studio for the pre-wedding photoshoot in the scenic hills of Rajgir.

"Di, got ready soon… we're getting late. Jiju and Saurav Anuraj with his team are waiting for you!" Rhea yelled sticking her head through Varushka's door for the fifth time.

The sky was still under a dark wrap. The crescent moon was yet to set. Varushka was feeling too sleepy to get ready for a journey of a hundred miles. The fairy tale theme for the shoot required a few shots at dawn.

"Almost done girl," Varushka replied applying the last touch up to her makeup. "They've made me get ready at this time of

the night as if we are going to shoot for a horror romance movie,"
she said to herself, blushing.

▼

When Varushka came out, she was looking like a Disney princess
in a red lace gown.

The dawn arrived with musical silence, the soul hearing a
melody that the ears could not fathom. A new day had come with
new possibilities; a fresh page yet to be written. The rising sun
sent shimmering rays over the placid lake, bestowing a golden
path from the shore to the horizon. Varushka blinked towards
the sun that brought her a day she was never promised, yet glad
to see. She let the moment sink in, soothe her from her core
right out to where the nascent rays touched her skin. This meant
a new beginning was possible. And possibilities meant hope.

"Hold each other's hands and take a stroll. Please gaze into
each other's eyes," Saurav directed the first ice-breaking pose
for the shoot.

"It's not happening guys. Something is missing…" Saurav
showed them some more photos to imitate. Yet it was still not
working well.

Saurav was continuously thinking about how to make them
pose.

"Hey guys, do you know dancing?" Saurav asked while
browsing through his mobile.

Varushka and Mitash looked at each other. "Yes!" both
replied in unison.

Saurav smiled and his twinkling eyes were screaming with
happiness as his idea was going to work now. He played the song,

'Do dil mil rahe hain… magar chupke chupke' and requested both of them to dance to it.

First, they hesitated. Varushka was a little nervous. Mitash too was not comfortable being in front of the camera. The ice between them had not yet broken.

However, as the shoot progressed, the nerves disappeared and the natural interaction between the couple was wonderful to see. Mitash gazed at her lovingly as she swirled around in her red gown, and the scene appeared breathtakingly romantic. While Varushka and Mitash were cherishing their fun-filled togetherness, Saurav was capturing these beautiful moments.

"Mitash, you have to kneel down and propose to her again. And when she places her hand in yours, you have to kiss her hand... then..." Saurav was instructing them for their further shots.

Mitash looked at Varushka, and lifted his brows for her permission. Mitash won her heart again with his chivalry. She blushed like a new bride and nodded 'yes'.

The touch of his lips on her hand gave her a cold shiver. Her face split into a shy smile. She swiftly looked away from him.

Mitash held her close to him, her back against his chest. She felt the warmth of his skin and his arm coiled around her waist.

She turned towards Mitash, leaned sideways, and rested her head on his left shoulder. She lay her right hand on his chest as Mitash was still holding her waist. The couple was now dancing together to another slow romantic song, as they began swaying back and forth. This was the first time she was experiencing a man's heart beating so close, under her palm.

Varushka moved her face up and she met his eyes. His slanted forehead was partially covered with his hair that the breeze had messed up. The unkempt hair was more natural and endearing. It made him look like a teenager. She was tempted to touch his hair, but resisted. The dark stubble on his cheeks made his nose look longer, more prominent, and his chin subtler. Varushka wished she could run her fingers over his dimpled cheek which was visible even when the sheer layer of beard was trying to hide it. His brow cast a shadow over his deep-set eyes – those intense eyes that she could never look away from now, especially when he laughed, resulting in adorable crinkles at the corners of his mouth.

Mitash held her shoulders softly and leaned in placing his lips on her forehead. It sent shivers down her spine. He pulled away a little, lingering just above her lips, looking at her. She held his gaze and held her breath. He let his nose touch hers. She could feel his warm breath on her face that was increasing her heartbeat, continuously. Her blood was rushing in multiple velocities. Something was taking away her control over her heart, and mind as well. She could feel her ears getting warm. She closed her eyes, sank her head into his chest and hid her face. Both hearts were beating in a rhythm. She was in a moment, loved and adored by the only man she had ever allowed herself to surrender to.

Their love chemistry and sentiments were perfectly captured by the lens.

Mitash was right, she thought, 'We don't decide with whom we fall in love with. It eventually happens.'

She was falling in love with Mitash!

The evening passed in amiable silence, both content to hear only the sound of wind in the trees and rustling of leaves; and each other's steady breathing.

Life like a Fairytale

With new hope, dreams and aspirations, Varushka flew with Mitash to a completely new country. It was the first flight in Varushka's life, that too an international one. She was excited, conscious and nervous as well. Travelling abroad had always been on her bucket list. However, this was something more special. She was not just going on a trip; she was going to set up her own family and abode, her *aashiyana* there. She felt butterflies in her stomach.

Sitting in the window seat, she was dreaming of what she would do once she reached her new home in Amsterdam. How she would decorate her bedroom and house, as she had always wanted. Where would she go on her honeymoon with Mitash? How would she respond when Mitash would try to come near her and get naughty? She had already bought sexy lingerie. The thoughts were already giving her goosebumps. Thinking she was asleep, Mitash covered her with a blanket. She soon rested her head on Mitash's shoulder with a shy smile and travelled to her wonderland as she saw Mitash's smiling face.

▼

When Mitash and Varushka landed in Amsterdam, the welcome they received was nothing less than a celebrity would receive in India. A troupe Mitash's Indians and European friends were dancing to dhol beats. They made Varushka and Mitash dance to some bhangra moves before walking towards the car.

Few more surprises were on the cards for Varushka. As Mitash's apartment's door opened, both were astounded to see a glass filled with rice kept at the door. One of Mitash's friends in a kurta held a plate with a little tea light, rose petals and red powder.

"Enrique, my best buddy and my flatmate!" Mitash introduced the French man to Varushka.

"And ze gorgeous lady is Varushka. *Bonjour* and *bienvenue,*" Enrique said with a smile and applied a tilak, followed by *aarti* and showering rose petals on them.

"Varushka, I have learnt a few of these rituals watching Bollywood movies. So don't mind if I make a mistake." Enrique winked. "You may enter our house as the new bride now," he added, pointing towards the glass.

Tilting the glass filled with rice using her right foot, Varushka stepped into a plate with red paint. After this, she walked into her new home leaving behind auspicious red footprints on the wooden flooring.

The apartment looked high-end and was done up newly, with an ethnic Indian style with a brass Buddha temple and a large painting of Lord Shiva. Mitash shared his two-bedroom apartment with Enrique, who had been his friend since university days. Enrique also worked at the same company as Mitash.

"Freshen up, you guys, and rest up for a bit. Then get ready for your party in the evening," Enrique said before leaving the newlywed's bedroom.

"Party! I'm so tired. I need to rest," Varushka said.

After a long journey of nineteen hours from Patna to Amsterdam via Delhi and Abu Dhabi, their bodies badly needed rest.

This welcome was overwhelming for Varushka in a foreign land, especially where she had no family and relatives. Everything seemed like a fairytale to her. A life she had absolutely wished for but had not imagined, had now begun. Her sparkling eyes were saying a lot as she hugged Mitash tightly. Mitash caressed her back lovingly.

▼

Mitash and his friends, along with their partners, met at La Oliva, one of the most happening restaurants at the city centre, for weekend parties. This time, however, it was even more special as Varushka was introduced to the troupe. There were about eight people from different parts of the world.

"This is Varushka," Mitash introduced her to his friends who were absent at the airport in the morning.

"So pretty," one of his friends mentioned.

Varushka blushed. She always felt confident of her looks, but never imagined to get a compliment from an Italian dude.

The lights were dim and the glittering chandeliers hanging from the ceiling with candles gave off a rustic, romantic vibe. Some were busy with the wine and dining, some were dancing to the groove of the techno music, and others were on the couch, laughing. All full of excitement as the weekend party was in full swing. Everyone at the party seemed to be having a good time. It was almost 3:30 a.m. when the hostess decided to call it a night. They realized they needed to get back to their apartments and bid each other good night.

▼

It was ten o' clock in the morning when the sun rays sent some warmth to her face filtered through the white sheer floral tulle voile curtains. Her first morning in Amsterdam.

Varushka smiled to herself and walked to the curtains where the light was coming in and parted them. To her surprise, it wasn't a long window, but a glass door. She slid it open and in front of her was a large-sized terrace, which she had always wanted. She slowly stepped into the terrace. The breeze blew her hair back and slowly her mouth opened and her eyes widened. She was mesmerized with the beauty of the surroundings. In front of her and across the street was the Amstel river. Two young girls and a boy were skating on the pavement, couples were walking hand in hand by the riverfront. There was also a small crowd of people singing along to a song being played by a bunch of musicians on the other side of the river bank. Below her terrace, people were eating, drinking and laughing.

It was like she was in Wonderland. It looked and felt magical. She just stood there for some time taking it all in.

She wanted to capture this beautiful scenario in her eyes, but soon she realized it was not a dream; she was going to stay here forever. At least until they planned to move to some other city or country.

▼

"Varushka…" Mitash brought her back from the dream to reality. "Breakfast is ready. We are waiting for you."

"Give me ten minutes!" she replied.

Mitash had made Al Forno in white sauce – a spicy Italian classic recipe, soup, Greek salad and fruit juice. Enrique had told her that Mitash was fond of cooking and every weekend they had something special for breakfast, lunch and dinner.

It was fun spending time together. Mitash, Varushka and Enrique soon became a family.

"First this!" Mitash placed an 8.3 x 11.7 inches silver envelope wrapped with a shimmery pink ribbon before her on the dining table.

Varushka was surprised to see that. "What's inside this?"

"A small gift for you. Open it and find out," he replied with a mysterious cheeky smile.

Varushka opened it and took out a paper that read 'Admission Offer'. She looked up at Mitash. Enrique too was looking at both of them, waiting for her reaction.

"See Varushka, it is time to chase your dream now. It is not always that easy to land a job here, specially with an Indian degree. So until you don't find a suitable job, you should take up this one year course that will enhance your skills and knowledge. This will help you to find your dream job too."

He made her speechless one more time. She hugged the man of her life. With the glittering wedding lights and music, she herself had forgotten what she had planned for her life. Her dreams. But to her surprise, Mitash, despite being so busy with his own work, juggling between his social life and personal life, was planning everything for Varushka to fulfil her dreams. She felt blessed having him in her life.

She remembered, few weeks before their wedding, Mitash had given her a couple of links and application forms and made her fill and sign them. But she really hadn't read any of them.

"Thank you so much!" she whispered into his ears, wishing to peck it.

"But, I have one more gift for you," he whispered back patting her back.

"Really? Where is that?" she almost screamed.

"Yep! And that you will get once Enrique and I reach office."

Mitash joined his office the very next day he reached Amsterdam. He had already been on a long vacation in India.

"Congratulations honey!" Enrique said with a smile as Varushka glared at him with questioning eyes.

▼

Here is your wish jar and your colourful dream papers. You must be wondering whether I have gone mad?

My answer is, 'No!'

Then you'll be thinking, "What are you gonna do with this stuff?"

My answer is, 'I know you have a lot to say. Many dreams and wishes hidden inside your heart. Many times you won't be able to say some or might not be able to share it with anyone. When I married you, I promised myself to fulfil all your wishes, even when you don't say them to me. At the same time, I know myself, it is neither easy nor possible to know your heart completely.

Giggling?

Listen. I have a trick for this.

These colourful papers are like your dream canvas. You gotta write your wishes, one on each paper, per day. Fold it and put it in the jar with the red lid with the red lock. Every weekend, I will unlock it and will try to make one of those wishes come true in the following week and then, when the wish is fulfilled, it will be transferred to another jar, that is one with the blue lid, kept in my cupboard.

Now don't be surprised, take a pen and start penning it all down.

Mitash

Varushka read the letter that she found with the jar kept on her dressing table. She rushed to his cupboard to look for the other jar.

Varushka was astonished by the thoughtful surprise. "Does this happen in real life?" she asked herself. She read the letter one more time and felt ridiculously happy. She had many fears regarding marriage earlier. Her life felt like a fairytale, hard to believe, but happening. "Touchwood!"

For a few seconds, she was unable to speak. Her eyes were filled with tears at the sweetness of Mitash's gesture. She really did not know what to say.

Sitting near the window, her newly found favourite place, with the gifts spread around her, she was still wondering which wish to write down first.

She took out her journal and read her wish list. Most of her wishes were crazy. Was it possible to go on a road trip across the country, that too driving herself when she didn't even know the country's driving rules? Hopefully make a world record, or even wearing a bikini in the cold icy water like a fish underwater. Yet, Mitash had urged her to share her list with him.

Whether it was possible or not. Whether it was easy or difficult, certainly it was extremely difficult to pen down.

▼

In the evening, Mitash was pleased to see a blue folded paper in the red jar.

Settling Down

The succeeding few days went away in the mist of new friends, fun and welcome parties that Varushka had no option but to be a part of.

Weekends were a bit different, waking up late, loitering around, visiting some places nearby or watching a movie, long walks in the evening, late-night discussions, entertainment sessions and long drives.

The best thing Varushka loved was to walk late at night along the banks of the Amstel river with both the men, and trying out new street food.

▼

After a few sodden weeks, everything began falling into a quiet routine. Starting the day with a morning walk and yoga, it went on with experimenting with her culinary skills. She also joined a weekend baking course and conducted all her gastronomical experiments for breakfast from Monday to Friday. The kitchen was Mitash's exclusive domain on weekends. Dinner, the three cooked together.

Some days, she felt she loved Mitash even more. Being with him with his showering affection was blissful. The way he listened to her made her feel valued and loved. His politeness, understanding, selflessness and taking interest in what really mattered to her had increased over the weeks.

Enrique, most of the time, reached home early. Varushka and Enrique would go for a walk around the block, have coffee and return home by the time Mitash arrived. Enrique talked about his school and college days. He also began teaching her French, besides sensitizing her to French and Dutch culture. In return, she would narrate to him the epics of rich Indian culture.

Though she had come so far from her home, her family, and her country, she did not feel strange. The two men had become an integral part of her life in these few weeks. Her new beautiful family.

The new place, the new lifestyle, and the new culture were slowly becoming Varushka's very own.

▼

"The office is sending Enrique and me to Rome for a week," Mitash announced as he entered the house. "I was thinking, why don't you join us?" he added looking at Varushka's puzzled face.

"Are you sure? You guys are going on an office trip!"

"We won't be working for more than five hours a day. In between, we'll have the weekend too," Enrique replied to convince her.

"Sounds great!" she screamed in excitement. "When are we leaving?"

"Tomorrow morning!" Mitash and Enrique said together.

"Are you serious?"

Varushka was worried how she would manage packing and dreaming about the forthcoming trip in a few hours? At home, they'd plan months before or at least weeks before a family trip. Once tickets were finalised, the itinerary was made, they'd shop, choose and try on dresses to take along, explore and read about the place. Then there was the long exciting wait for the trip to begin.

More than packing, she was worried about not having time to feel the excitement. All of a sudden, she remembered something, killing her excitement.

"I can't…" she said unwillingly as the feeling of sadness appeared on her face.

"But why?" Enrique asked.

"What would you do here alone? Even your classes are not going to start for another two weeks!" a disappointed Mitash said sadly.

"Some other problem.."

"What?"

Varushka looked at Mitash, then at Enrique. "Can't say… something personal," and turned to Enrique.

Enrique got the hint.

"Oh… I have to make a call. Join you guys later."

Still, Varushka was quiet.

"Tell me. Now no one else is here," he said and sat next to her.

"My periods are due after three days," she replied embarrassed, without looking at him.

At first, he was not sure what he had heard. "You mean your menstrual dates?"

"Yup!"

"Is that an issue?. Oh god, you are speaking like a girl who is gonna get her first period. I will get enough sanitary napkins for you and that too those that stay all day long. Come on, Varushka!" he laughed.

But what about the cramps, pain and menstrual syndrome?

"Phew... you have no idea how much it pains. I can't even stand or sit. I need to rest even after taking a pain-killer."

Mitash was staring at her with wide eyes.

"Really? Never heard this."

"I am sure, you never asked anyone. By the way, it doesn't happen with everyone, but many experience pain like me."

"Isn't there any solution?" he asked. "Must be!" he added before she could say anything. "You start packing and leave everything else to me."

Mitash kissed her on her forehead and left to inform Enrique.

See Italy and Die

"I can't believe I am here. Heaven! It is such a beautiful place," Varushka screamed popping her head out of the window of their two-bedroom service apartment in Rome.

"Yeah. Finally! Should we sit down?" Mitash called Enrique too. "So here is the plan. First, we go skydiving tomorrow morning. Then Enrique wants to take you for an underwater life experience. So we will then head to Sardinia, a beautiful island in the Mediterranean Sea. After that, we will come back to Rome. On Monday, till we complete our office work and return, Varushka can explore the city on her own. In the evening, Enrique and I will join you to check out the wildering nightlife."

The three tired souls fell on their bed. Varushka began recounting the plan for the next seven days in her head and dreamt of a thrilling day next morning.

It was their first day there. The mere thought of falling off a height of thousands of metres and then landing on the ground on your feet seemed to be wild enough. Enrique had already finished the multiple online paperwork on behalf of the three, where one signs their whole life away, giving the onus of any liability in case of a catastrophe in the form of injury or death. Before they had signed the disclaimer, they had seen a video and had taken note of all the safety guidelines accountable for their lives.

This may seem to be the hardest part, where you're gambling with your life. Varushka always wanted to do this. She had many more adventures in her wish list (those she hadn't dropped in the wish jar yet). Although now, when the moment was right in front of her, she was scared.

"You don't have to step back, Varushka. Embrace your fear factor and trust me, you will feel as if you have been reborn," Enrique encouraged her, reading her expressions.

"Mitash is scared of heights, even though he is going to do this for the first time," he chuckled.

Mitash nodded without looking at them, busy however, diverting his mind from freaking out by solving his all-time favourite puzzle. Varushka admired his guts and looked at the sky. It was clear, blue and sunny with a cool breeze.

The instructor gave five minutes of training to the skydiving virgins – cross arms, head back, knees bent, jump. One tap on the shoulder to open arms. Second, to bring arms to chest as the parachute opens. Knees bent for landing. Questions?

"I have..." asked a visibly scared Mitash, "How many jumps have you overseen before... this one?" Mitash questioned in a quivering voice.

The other two couldn't control their laughter. The instructor smiled. The instructor was familiar with the fear of first-timers. "I have done more than five thousand and fifty jumps. I have lost count. Have full faith. You are in safe hands. Nothing will happen to you."

In the aeroplane boarding area, the Roman sun greeted them with ferocity as their hands grasped raw metal and their feet took them up the ladder into the cabin.

Soon the troop was in. The door closed. Varushka was no longer freaking out. They were off. Enrique was an expert diver. He decided to dive solo and the other two were jumping in tandem with an instructor besides three cameramen. Crammed on the benches, cross-legged, facing each other's backs, Mitash asked, "So guys, how's the feeling right now?"

At several thousand feet, Varushka closed her eyes. Her heart was now beating fast and she was a little anxious.

Varushka had always wondered what it would be like to fly. As a kid, running through the yard with her arms spread out, she used to pretend that she was flying an aeroplane through the air. She also simulated weird engine noises whenever she would make a turn or go into a steep dive. Flying through the air was her dream. However, when she wished to be a pilot, it was not acceptable to her family. Well, now she was getting to fly for the first time, and it wasn't flying in an aeroplane. It was by jumping out of one, like an eagle.

"Still like a dream!" she replied to Mitash after trying to overcome her fear by weakly smiling and looking out of the window. First Enrique jumped out of the plane, roaring aloud as if he was going to a rave party. Varushka was fascinated by his confidence. The sight looked surreal from the aeroplane window.

Next was Varushka's turn.

"Sit on my lap," said her instructor. "We must get ready. Bend your knees."

She had to obey. From behind, the instructor pulled the straps until the rubber scraped her skull. Varushka hugged her arms against her chest and cranked her head back, making the shackles around her thighs tighten further. The harness compresses her pelvis and ribcage and they stumbled out of the plane.

There was no anxiety and no tension in the free clouds. She could feel the cool air on her face with the speed of more than a hundred miles per hour, as if it was welcoming her.

"Now," commanded the instructor, "and don't forget to smile for the camera." At that moment, devoid of pain, grief, and worry, she looked out upon the landscape of the beautiful earth below and was surprised to feel complete peace within herself with that action. Varushka was suddenly carried back up in the air.

She squealed in excitement. *"Yes! I did my first jump. Yes!"*

She was screaming her heart out with thrill and joy. However, the air whipped away her voice, deafening her own ears to her own screams of joy.

The experience was nothing like she had imagined. She didn't feel as though she was falling. Spinning upwards and backwards was soon transformed as floating in the quiet air. Still so high, she felt as if she was a beautiful bird that she had always dreamt of being. Stretching out her arms, feeling the sky run through her fingers felt like scorched cotton candy; she could now see the world in a whole new way. Soaring across the sky with the freeing feeling of liberation.

Varushka waved at the people on the ground and saw them waving back with amusement. It was the best moment of her life, intoxicating her mind and soul. At that moment, while descending, she felt she owned the world.

'Skydiving is something which one must try once before dying,' said her new Instagram feed.

▼

After a road trip to Civitavecchia followed by an overnight journey by ferry, early the next morning, they reached Stintino in the northwest corner of the island of Sardinia, ready for another amazing encounter of their lives.

"It is a whole new world underwater and you ought to see it before you die. If you want to make it even more thrilling, you can also try swimming with those big fish in the sea or even with a shark," the scuba diving instructor closed his brief training before diving into the water.

"Enrique, this time Mitash is gonna step down into the water first," Varushka said giving a mischievous smile to her husband. The previous day, Mitash was so scared that he refused to jump from the plane.

"He is scared of heights, not of depth. Am I right, my dear Mitash?" Enrique fondly teased him.

After Enrique and Varushka had landed on the earth, they had waited for Mitash for a long time and found him missing. Running all over the field, they searched every corner of the area. Enrique had began fighting with the Centre Admin and Varushka was almost in tears. In a bit, a relaxed composed happy Mitash appeared wearing his headphones listening to music. A relieved Enrique and Varushka dug out the whole story from Mitash. Thereafter, they did not miss any chance to pull his leg.

Varushka looked at the calmness of the sea. The idea of leaving the world she had always known, and entering into something far mysterious was undoubtedly daunting. There were mixed emotions of the excitement and an unknown fear. Then she looked at her instructor who was confidently and proudly narrating his previous experiences. She looked at Mitash and Enrique, listening to the instructor keenly. Once again, she looked at the sea. "It would be as great an experience as yesterday and I am not scared at all," she convinced herself and smiled.

Within the next few minutes, she was inside the water, along with the instructor, Mitash and Enrique. Soon, every sound would be unheard in this aqua world. As she slowly sank down, life underwater seemed to be going in slow-motion, tranquil and unreal. There was no fear anymore, only sheer awe and wonder.

Being submerged under water, she was surprised to note that there was absolutely no gravitational pull, despite the heavy weights and gear she was wearing. She wanted to explore the greater depths of the sea. Swimming down a little deeper left Varushka feeling serene and mellow. She even forgot to breathe. She forgot her own existence. In the depths of the Tyrrhenian Sea, the life she saw – existing and moving – was totally magical.

The world slowed as she tried to savour every moment. Everything moved at a snail's pace. She suddenly saw the sheer amount of wildlife, uncountable fish dancing in their impressive formation, and candy-hued corals swaying underneath like a colourful Monet creating an incredible feeling. Crabs were crawling across the sea floor, as the colourful parrotfish appeared all of a sudden, eating algae off the coral reefs. The discoveries were endless.

It was more beautiful than she had imagined and the tranquility was unparalleled.

The only sound she could hear was that of her own breath. When she looked around, she was amazed at the infinite length her eyes could capture. She was in awe of its sheer magnificence and just wanted time to stand still to explore the deep waters as much as she could. She wanted to stay there and take it all in until her thoughts were interrupted by Enrique's waving gesture, indicating to get to his side. She then swam back, reaching him.

Mitash and the instructor were waiting for the pictures to be taken as their cylinders were indicating that it was time to get back to the upper world now. They posed and took pictures together, moving around plants and rocks, swimming after schools of fish.

Exploring nature is like experiencing the power that rejuvenates your inner self again. It was like a dream you do not want to wake up from; swimming with a shoal of bream, plants tickling your body with the smallest touch and the limitless vision of water all around you, profoundly impact you with its minute details.

If it were up to me, I would want to live this dream again and again and again – read her latest Instagram feed flooded with her underwater life memories.

▼

It was Monday and they were back in Rome. For the next five days, Varushka woke up late, once Mitash and Enrique left for their office. After a rich European breakfast, she explored the city on her own. In the evenings, they all gathered at a common point. They explored some rides on public buses, trains, ate together, enjoyed late night parties and danced till they... oops, Varushka dropped.

It was not like any of her other trips. This trip was intoxicating. Italy, a country best known for zest for life is not one to rush through at all. Roman ruins are around every nook and corner. The Colosseum, the Ponte Vecchio, Grand Piazzas, fountains and outdoor cafés dot the city. They just beg you to sit down for a few hours and soak in the ambience.

▼

It was past eight in the night, when they returned to the hotel. Exhausted, Varushka wanted to just get in and collapsed on the bed. Varushka delved into her baggage for a while and finally got into her blue shorts and white tank top.

"Don't you want to change?" Varushka asked Mitash tossing his grey boxer and a black t-shirt at him. Mitash shook his head. "Later."

Varushka took a shower and got ready to cuddle into bed.

"Feel like a drink?" Mitash asked, disrupting the to-do list that was gradually unfolding in her head. She looked at the stylish bottle in his hand with the 'Absolut Elyx' labelled on it. Varushka surrendered. The thought of leaving Rome next night made her want to grab hold of every precious moment she could get.

"Why not?" she replied and he served her one of his best Patiala pegs.

They sipped their drinks in the dim, romantic string fairy lights.

"I need music," she demanded. Mitash opened his laptop and set it to her much-loved Punjabi track. It made her think back of their pre-wedding photo shoot. They drank, laughed and teased each other late into the night. In a while, she switched off the lights and lit a few candles.

"Do you want to dance?" Varushka invited, flashing a romantic smile. Mitash, fixing their third round, seemed to find it difficult to turn down the request from his assertive newlywed wife.

He smiled, took a step forward and bowed, holding his glass in his left hand. She gave her left hand to him and came out of the bed. They both gulped down almost a quarter of their newly-filled glasses in a single shot before placing their glasses on the nearby coffee table.

Placing her hands on his shoulders, they danced silently. He smelt good. His spicy aroma was appealing. Slowly, she moved her hands up to his neck and rested her head on his chest. Her bare cheek was cool from the breeze coming through the window, yet his beating heart brought all the blaze of fire to rush to her cheeks, making it warm with a glowy tint.

A few minutes later, Mitash attempted to say something, but couldn't say as all the vodka finally hit them. Whether it was the music, alcohol or the candle lights, Varushka got suddenly possessive and pulled her husband impossibly closer to her. She moved her head forward to kiss him. He moved his head backwards and successfully avoided her lips saying, "Ssshhh… you are drunk." and swallowed one more shot.

Then slowly, he took a step back and she looked up confused, feeling slightly dejected. But within a second, he twirled her around and pushed his front into her back, still moving slowly side to side. He scrubbed his nose on the side of her slender suave neck and grinned. She smelled sensuous, like cinnamon and meadow-fresh mint. His lips against her skin, and his strong arm across her upper shoulder made her feel protected as they twisted and turned with a melody no one else could hear.

Varushka was then facing him. Slowly pushing one of her loose tendrils behind her ear, he smiled a sincere smile. She looked up at him in embarrassment and awe. She had trout pout lips – sumptuous, kiss-inspiring and satin soft. Her face shimmering in the moonlight and her eyes gleaming with an emotion so intense, she couldn't even empathise with what he thought. She was beautiful, as always. He held the back of her neck with firm fingers. Mitash breathed harder, matching the rhythm of Varushka's now erratic breaths. He brought his head forward. His lips were parted slightly, blowing warm air on her neck.

She shuddered with desire as an enthralling fire lit her body. She lingered close to his lips for just a second, looking at him, and then her lips touched his. She closed her eyes. Mitash fervently kissed her back. It sent shivers down her spine. Her mouth slipped from his lips to his cheeks, then his ear and then his neck, leaving a trail of wet kisses. She rubbed her face against his chest and he grunted.

Mitash pulled away and lay down on his back, Varushka moved with him, as if she was being drawn to him by some mystic force. Mitash drew her towards him and she hugged him as tight as she could and kissed him all over, more ferociously. Varushka surrendered herself, melting in his arms. Mitash let his hand slip over her neck, under her tank top and stroked her back. He then held her waist with one arm, moving his face down to her thigh, her knee, and further down to her ankle. They kissed again. His lips were soft and gentle, still persuasive. He then planted his mouth between her thighs and began sucking and nibbling her, that drove her wild into a place of passion she had never experienced before.

"Mitash!" Varushka moaned, engulfed in Mitash's love making and his spicy fragrance spread through her.

Varushka wanted to say something, but struggled with finding the right words to express her emotions. Mitash's tongue dug deeper depths into her. She dug her nails into his bare back as he pulled back to gasp some air.

She opened her eyes to look at him. His eyes were still closed. Varushka pulled his face up and their lips touched again. Their eyes met as she took in Mitash as her lover. She smiled at him longingly as he moved forward to kiss her. Her lips moved against his, sucking, nibbling. She kissed him back passionately. He continued kissing her. His tongue made its way into her mouth, wheedling her to open it further, let him in. Her tongue automatically pushed itself into his mouth.

Mitash moaned and exclaimed, "Oh god!"

Varushka then twirled facing him. She placed her hand on his chest, running her fingers up to his shoulder, neck and then back. She then tore his shirt open, pushed him on his back, sat on his waist. She leaned in to kiss him again. Varushka flowed her fingers freely on his back, feeling his soft skin and tensed muscle, lifted his arm above his head and began nibbling and kissing him from his chest to navel and back. As he kept groaning, "Varushka please, Varushka. Oh Varushka!"

She moved her fingers up his stomach, to his bushy chest. She held a few strands and played with them running her finger over his neck and shoulders. Varushka slipped from his lips to his neck. She nibbled at it, causing Mitash to quiver. He grunted. His fingers found the skin below her neck. He stroked her back down to her waist, placed his palm down on her stomach. Her back arched up to snuggle softly against his chest. She bent forward, balancing herself on her knees, kissing him again.

He didn't stop, neither did Varushka. Their bodies touched and shared heat. Varushka held his face with her palms while she explored his mouth with hers. They played with each other's tongues. Varushka sucked his lower lips and he groaned.

Mitash slid his hand towards her back and unhooked her bra. Her bared breasts in front of a man, for the first time, turned her red. She tried to hide from him. He pushed her hands aside and glided his hands all over her body, her back, caressing her breasts, stomach and reached for the waist of her shorts. He pulled on her blue string that held her cotton shorts in place. Before he threw the shorts on the floor, Varushka felt his hands tracing every inch of her leg, in the process of pulling it off.

Varushka pulled him towards her as their lips locked. Their hands were exploring each other's bodies. Their mouths followed the movement of their hands. Mitash rested on his back, Varushka plonked on him with her legs on either side. She arched her body back. Her eyes shut, her nails jabbing his body.

Both down to their naked vulnerable truths. They began discovering each other's bodies. Their mouths followed the movement of their hands. Varushka was then overpowered by Mitash who rested her on her back, spread her legs and explored her womanhood with his tounge.

This drove Varushka even crazier as she arched her body back and forth into Mitash's face. This time her nails dug deeper into his back as she exploded her undiscovered passionate pleasure over his face, creating slight bloody scratch marks on his tight toned back, marking him as her man.

Mitash jolted back saying, "Aaahh..."

She grabbed him to her lips and kissed him with her wildest passion and dropped into a deep pleasurable satisfied slumber.

▼

Next morning, when Varushka woke up, her head was feeling heavy. The previous night, she had been four Patiala drinks down.

She got out of bed and looked around. The crumpled bedsheet, pillows and cushions were strewn all over the mattress; some on the floor. The blue shorts and black jeans lay on each other. Her white tank top and underwire bra hung carelessly on different sides of the large bed's head-support. After a careful assessment of the aftermath of last night's love-making scene, a smile crept over her face, turning her cheeks red with heat. After all, her wait for the first night was worth it.

'I was right, he was giving us time to be comfortable all these months,' she thought.

"But where is Mitash? I didn't expect him to be up so early," she whispered to herself, wrapping her robe around her.

She heard loud voices outside. She went out of the room, following the sound. She saw Enrique just about going out, fuming, red in the face.

"Enrique?" she called him.

He didn't reply and was gone.

He must not have heard her or gone somewhere in urgency, she thought and then decided to freshen up before starting her day. It was Friday, their last day in Rome. Enrique and Mitash would finish their office work sooner as they were permitted to leave early from office.

Mitash hurriedly got dressed saying he would speak to her about Enrique later.

▼

Varushka did a zig-zag sightseeing of Piazza Colonna and its massive column of Marcus Aurelius to Via dei Condotti. Thereafter she settled comfortably at a table at Antico Caffè Greco, one of the oldest coffee houses in all of Italy. She dined well, ordering Caprese Salade and Veal Saltimbocca. She then checked the time. It was just 11 a.m. Mitash had asked her to meet Enrique and him at Fontana di Trevi at 1:30 p.m.

It is like a wishing fountain, where people throw coins in the water. The tradition behind throwing coins over their shoulders comes from the legend that a coin thrown into the fountain will ensure a return to Rome. This tradition also dates back to ancient Romans who often threw coins in the water to make the gods of water favour their journey or help them get back home safely.

Varushka threw a coin and turned. "Why did you throw three coins?" she asked Mitash. "Only one is enough to return to Rome," she said and winked.

"The title of the movie *Three Coins in the Trevi Fountain* was on my mind," he replied.

Varushka was confused listening Mitash. She hadn't seen the movie, nor heard the name. She simply had followed what the guide explained to the other tourists here.

The second legend was the inspiration behind the film *Three Coins in the Trevi Fountain.* It claims that you should throw three coins into the fountain. The first coin guarantees your return to Rome, the second coin if you're seeking love, and the third will ensure wedding bells!

By the time the three reached Piazza Campo Marzio, the sun had nearly set. Varushka's legs had given out at last. Varushka sunk into an outdoor table and chair at Ristorante Boccondivino. "Let's dine here, so that we rest at the hotel for a while before we leave for the airport," a tired Varushka suggested holding the menu card. Varushka was craving to eat and sleep, but at the same time, not wanting the night to end.

"Life is beautiful. Yes. To me, it is indeed," Varushka murmured looking at the graffiti on the wall on the opposite street.

As melodramatic as it might sound, once I had witnessed the beauty of Italy with my own eyes, and felt transformed by it, I knew that it was possible for someone to breathe their last, happy and content in the memory of such a place. "See Italy and Die."

Varushka's Insta feed on the last day of her honeymoon trip concluded.

A Ten Day Thief is caught
One Day

More than a month passed by.

Once again, everyone returned to their daily routines. Varushka had started going to her classes. Mitash and Enrique were busy with work. Since Varushka was occupied with her studies, college and new friends, the frequency of outings dropped. The city was no longer a strange place for Varushka.

▼

The last lecture of the day ended at around three o'clock in the afternoon. Mitash and Enrique were on an official trip to London and were to be returning home that night. They had been gone for a week. Varushka had been feeling that she had been away from Mitash for years, and waiting for few more hours seemed difficult now.

She packed her stuff and bid goodbye to her friends. Suddenly there was chaos all around there. Everyone running towards the vestibule. Panicked, Varushka called her friends and together they ran following the others. However, the scenario there was something else.

A boy from the same university was standing there. His hands were holding a small velvet box. Six of his friends (they seemed to be) were serenading the violin, guitar and other musical instruments. Another batch of eight friends were holding an A4 size red paper with different letters inked with white on it. Varushka read it, 'M A R R Y M E ?' and then there was a beautiful surprised girl, trying to absorb the moment completely, a little confused and filled with mixed emotions. The girl was still trying to make out what it was. The boy rapidly changed his position from standing to kneeling on the ground with a ring in his hand. The girl's eyes widened and her mouth gaped as the boy sputtered, "Iva, will you marry me?"

The girl, nervous, diverted her gaze, hugged herself, starting to rock back and forth on her feet. *"Ik hou van je you* (I love you)... Aldert." She turned her head back towards the boy, met his eyes. The crowd rejoiced to and screamed, *"Hoera...* (Hooray)" as their lips locked with each other with her reply, *"Ik doe* (I do)."

As they hugged tightly, snowflakes began falling, forming a beautiful white carpet. It seemed as if nature was blessing the couple.

Varushka stretched out her arms experiencing the first snowfall of her life. Varushka then crossed her arms and hugged herself. Suddenly she felt she was missing something. It was Mitash. The weather was full of romance and was making her miss him even more.

A smile crept on Varushka's face. She gasped some air, "Just a few more hours."

▼

There is beauty in the winters in Europe. The sprinkling down of snow from a grey sky that floats to the ground with grace and elegance so pure, as if a fairy has sprinkled her dust over the entire world. Colours are brighter against the pure white blanket that spreads as far as the eye can see. The houses, their chimneys, and trees become an art sculpture taking on new forms.

The air smells pure and fresh. Everything seems quieter and almost muffled. There is a sense of serenity in the atmosphere. This adds to the eeriness and quietness. Standing on the terrace, Varushka was witnessing the snowfall covering the city. She stuck her tongue out trying to taste the falling snowflakes from the sky. Few fell gently on her face, tickling the end of the nose, making it red. Her fingers and toes soon felt numb. The icy air whistled around her ears, causing her skin to tingle and sting. Everything was so beautiful.

Varushka went indoors. She then closed her eyes crossing her body with her arms and snug inside her many layers of clothes. Nothing could spoil the overwhelming feeling of hugging her man. The urge to feel his warm breath transported her into another world. Her ears got warm and cheeks turned red as the thought crossed her mind. Cuddling with Mitash and both kissing desperately was melting away all snow in her imagination. She yearned to make deeper intense love. She felt like reaching out and hugging him right now at the thought.

It made her smile to think that Mitash would be with her after three hours. It was for the first time after her marriage that she was away from him for even a single day. She was going crazy with every passing second.

Before his flight, Mitash had called her which made a part of her happy with the news that Enrique had to stay back a few more weeks and visit his family in France before returning home as his father wasn't in the best of health.

▼

For the first time, they'd be alone in the house. She prepared his favourite meal with carrot and walnut cake for dessert. She decorated the dining table with Jasmine aromatic candles. Still, there was so much time to wait. She decided to adorn her sexy lingerie which was yet to be used and decorate, their room with his favourite flowers.

"Where did I keep the new bedsheet?" she murmured while looking for stuff inside the wardrobe. After a few minutes of struggle, she found it deep inside.

"Aha… here it is…" she pulled it out in a jiffy. Along with it, a few things came tumbling out. Among that was a leather file. Varushka wondered why the file was there.

"This file must be here by mistake. Let me open and see if there are some important documents that Mitash might need," she said flipping the sides. She unzipped it and found it was a leather diary.

She was again baffled and puzzled. "Whose diary is it? Should I open it or not?"

Her curiosity took the better of her and she decided to flip the pages to find out whom the diary belonged to. It appeared to be someone's personal journal written in black ink. Varushka loved the lettering so much that she kept flipping pages even without reading it. More than two hundred pages were inscribed.

Her eyes read some keywords like 'India, Proposal, Ring, Marriage, Rome, Wishlist Jar, Love, Varushka, Mitash.'

There was only one interpretation possible of these keywords in her comprehension. The writer had to be Mitash.

It became obvious to her. Again a question popped in her head, 'A journal is personal and private to its author, but why has he hid it here when she never touches any of his documents or files without his permission? Or has it gone missing and Mitash wasn't able to find it?'

She decided to go through the initial pages. He had mentioned few words like new home, housewarming ceremony, travel to India, parents pressurizing for marriage. She thought of the date when she had met Mitash in Patna.

It read,

'It was she. Only she. I knew it from the very time I saw her on her 'arranged date' with a guy in the café. Her family was sitting restlessly with the guy's family and that was the moment she made me turn my head and decide that if I am going to marry, she is the one and could be my right match. Today when she accepted my invitation, I am cent per cent assured. Waiting for her final reply.'

Varushka jumped to their surprise Rome honeymoon trip date page.

'One more step towards fulfilling the promise I made to Varushka and myself. I am excited and happy that I have been able to fulfill four to five wishes from her wish list and few which she didn't even put in the Wish Jar, but, had mentioned to me in our initial meetings. Although I am always scared of heights, I thought to give it a try for her sake. At least she experienced something she always dreamt of. Although, once again, I couldn't dare to do

it myself. Everything was a blur to my eyes at that height. I was extremely scared. People don't expect this from a man, but I had to step back. I have no regrets as it was all for Varushka.'

There was also an image attached to the same page. The group photo of Mitash, Varushka, Enrique and their scuba diving instructor underwater.

"God, I am missing him even more now. He says it, but he expresses his love for me in all other possible ways, that I can't even imagine how much he loves me sometimes," she said.

She read each page that she thought was related to her and relived all those moments that she had spent with him. She felt a sense of déjà vu, reliving the sense of romance all over again.

She wanted to know more about his feelings for her.

'It is not easy for me to live my two lives together. It's a dilemma, whether I should tell her or not. It is not letting me live peacefully. It's her right to know and I am doing injustice with him too. I am waiting for the right time... to pluck up the required courage.

God, give me the strength to reveal the truth.'

She could now feel every single word pound in her chest amplifying in an echo. A sense of a strange fear swathed her. Then there was the big part as she turned more pages that turned her life completely upside down. Her fingers and body began shivering and shaking wildly, as her pulse started raising her heartbeat and heat well-up tears in her eyes.

She gulped and swallowed hard to constrict an emotional choke to re-read...

'Enrique, I know you are hurting and are in tremendous pain with my actions these days... I have had to only show love to her affirming her as my wife. I have as I promised to you, not misused

her virginity. I assure you, nothing has happened... I forever need you... Always my Enrique... my love... my strength... my backbone and my true life partner. I beg you never to leave me as I don't know what I will do to myself without you.'

It was not merely hard but seemed impossible to believe what she had just read. All the past memories were flashing before her eyes and she was getting different gists and intentions behind Mitash's actions. Shock waves turned her into a lifeless body. She did not even realize the doorbell ringing or her mobile buzzing since long until Mitash entered the house with the help of a spare key. Mitash frowned with worry seeing Varushka on the floor near his wardrobe; file, papers, clothes and other stuff scattered around.

"You okay?" he asked.

Varushka did not respond.

"You don't look too good. What's wrong?"

Still, she did not show sign of any emotion. It was as if someone had cast a spell on her.

Mitash couldn't understand what had happened. The decoration on the dining table and the room with candles and flowers, aroma of his favourite food were narrating another story. But Varushka seemed numb. Mitash gripped her shoulders and shook her out of a trance with a jerk.

"Talk to me..." he said heatedly.

Varushka did not respond. She simply looked at him and silently handed over the diary and photographs she had found inside.

Mitash felt his throat constricted and choked. His chest began thumping hard and his face and whole body began burning.

"Mitash, what is this?" she questioned in a low lost tone. "Answer me…" she then shrieked.

An unknown force was pulling her down, not only her legs, but her whole body. She found it difficult to stand. She knelt down in front of him, looking up at his face.

"Mitash, for god's sake, say something!" she yelled.

He kept avoiding eye contact.

"Is it a joke or the truth?" Varushka pleadingly tried to press on, though her voice hardly held together, each word fragmented from the other. Her left hand supported her body against her thighs, while her right hand came to her forehead, rubbing across her face, in an attempt to make sense of what was happening.

Mitash looked at her. She met his eyes, dull and vacant.

"Is everything that you wrote true, Mitash?" Varushka urged again. She couldn't look away from his eyes, those hollow brown shells, devoid of all emotions. Dead. She erupted, "Just say it. *Speak up dammit!"*

Varushka could see Mitash's chest rising and falling as he took deep breaths. The only sign of his existence.

Her brown eyes pleaded. She spoke again quietly, "Just say it once… whatever you wrote is not true…"

Varushka observed his eyes filling up with tears. His lips trembled to say something which never came out. Appearing defeated for some reason, the words were at the tip of his tongue, refusing to exit his mouth. His voice choked. He sat on his knees in front of her. He held her face. Their noses touched. For the first time, she felt empty and uncomfortable being so close to him. She experienced a mystic energy repelling her away from him.

"I am not kidding, Varushka. Each word of what you read is true. I wanted to tell you my truth for a long time."

After struggling with his inner voice, with a great difficulty, he admitted the truth.

He couldn't look into her eyes when he finally admitted his ongoing relationship with Enrique since university.

A force hit her heart. Her heart sank in. Her pulse slowed down as she couldn't empathize with his emotional response. Several questions sprouted in her mind, but she could not say anything.

It again went completely silent for about twenty long seconds.

She felt her body suddenly turn cold. She pushed him away from her with all her power and stood up. Hundreds of questions were badgering her mind, along with shock, rage, humiliation and disbelief.

"Mitash, why the fuck did you marry me?" she yelled.

She grabbed her head, pulling her hair, unable to sense what was going on exactly.

"Why did you lie that you liked me and proposed to me? Why did you fake everything since then, that fake love, fake happiness… lie… everything is fake and a bloody lie…"

"Listen to me once, Varushka. I will explain everything. Everything you read was not fake. Give me a chance to explain… please, Varushka…"

Varushka left Mitash on the floor – cold, dead, without saying a word.

▼

Varushka found herself sitting in one corner of the terrace, clenching her knees to her chest, with her head resting on the fence. Their whole relationship flashed before her, piece by piece, digging harder into her emotional wounds.

The Confrontation

At times, when you see or feel something real, it fixes you and you want to quit pretending. You feel like an idiot, a charlatan. It makes you want to escape from everything that has deserted you, whether it is innocently and harmlessly so, or something more serious like your disfunctional marriage.

This had happened to her.

Lying on the bed, silently, she put on her top and slipped her body under the blanket in the locked bedroom.

Even the warmth of the blanket couldn't make her sleep. She flipped the sides a few more times before throwing the covers away. Scenes from her first conversation with Mitash, his marriage proposal, their engagement and wedding kept playing out in front of her eyes. The trip they had made together to Italy flashed before her eyes. She had really enjoyed herself. They had giggled and chuckled the way couples in love do.

It was 3 a.m. on the breezy December night in Amsterdam and she found herself needing peace by returning to her terrace on the twenty-fifth floor. A cold wind blew, causing a mystic tune playing through the apartments.

▼

Varushka woke up after a catnap and tried to make sense of her surroundings as she lay in bed.

'My bedroom,' she recollected. Still lying on her stomach, she then got out of her bed and unlocked the door to see Mitash as he slept with his mouth slightly open on the living room couch. He was wearing the same red t-shirt and grey pyjamas which she had bought for him. His entire body was wrapped snugly around a pillow that she wished to exchange places with.

Varushka looked at him long and hard, unable to make peace with the fact that it was the same guy she had thought she could never run out of a conversation with. It was partially true, given that they still had a lot to talk and discuss. Their conversation had now grown silent or turned into a monologue, since the previous evening. The content more poignant.

She wondered how everything has changed overnight. Someone she longed for a few hours back, now seemed like a complete stranger. Among many principles she clung to in life, the inviolability of marriage was something she strongly believed in. That was the reason seeing another guy wasn't even a thought in her head. She stood in silence that very moment, shuffling her feet in embarrassment and pain.

Every event that had happened in the last few months was flashing before her. This time she could even remember the behind the scene stories that she never earlier realized. She understood why 'a friend' Enrique was still staying with Mitash even though he had got married. Why Enrique was part of their breakfasts, dinners, evening drives and shopping trips as well.

Why on many weekends, instead of giving privacy to the newly married couple, Enrique and Mitash would have some important work, or travel out of town for a few hours.

Why was she the one who had a blackout and slept off early every night during their Rome trip and the next morning she'd find Mitash and Enrique sleeping in the same room. And when she'd asked the reason, the regular excuse was, "We were partying until the morning and dozed off." Sometimes it would be, "We were busy discussing office work and passed out." Now she realized why Enrique didn't respond to her greeting on the last day of their Rome trip and why he was upset with Mitash.

Varushka hated every part of it now. She did not want to face either Mitash or Enrique even for a fraction of a second.

She got into the shower, taking her time shampooing her hair. The warm water felt good against her scalp. She got dressed for class and left home quietly without disturbing Mitash. It was still early and she didn't see many people on her way to the university.

She entered the campus cafeteria, got some coffee, a slice of toast and a piece of cheese. She took her plate to a table beside the window. She looked out at the murky blue sky waiting for sunshine to make it livelier. The day now appeared dull like a funeral chapel.

"Hey Varushka, how's it going? Up so early?" her friend Sophie commented as she sat down opposite her, also looking out of the window.

Varushka stared into her coffee cup for a long moment, and Sophie repeated her question. Finally, she looked up with a forced tiny smile, "I am sorry," she said. "I was thinking." Her voice was soft, and a bit strained, like someone had hit her in her gut.

"I get distracted a lot these days. I am sorry," she replied.

"It is still 7:30 a.m… so early…" Sophie remarked raising one of her eyebrows.

"So are you."

"Fair enough! I have to finish the assignment early; we're planning to go out for Oliver's birthday later in the evening. Are you coming?"

Varushka hesitated. "Actually… I don't…"

"C'mon… you should definitely hang out with us tonight. You haven't met everyone since a long time," Sophie said. Sophie spotted someone entering the caféteria and called out, waving her hand, "Hey Richard, here! I am coming!"

"It's going to be a lot of fun tonight. You should totally come," Sophie said finishing the last sip of her coffee.

Varushka smiled. "I will try to make it."

"Fun!" Varushka said softly. "My life is already a circus. They made fun of me. Made fun of my desires, my dreams – my life," she said to herself.

Varushka checked the time on her phone. No messages or missed calls. She hated when that happened, particularly when she was disturbed and feeling lonely. She kept her phone away on mute for a few hours, expecting a call or text. Maybe he was still asleep, she reasoned.

"Let's go," Sophie said, shaking her out of her thoughts.

Varushka got up, and the world swayed. She nearly lost her balance. She was more drained and exhausted than she had believed. She placed her palm flat on the table for support, staying very still, waiting for this sensation to go.

"Are you alright?" Sophie asked, studying her face.

"Yes… yes." She didn't elaborate. She breathed out deliberately before picking up her bag. "Ready!"

They walked out of the caféteria together, towards their class. They were walking fast and Varushka was losing energy. She was feeling so lonely. She missed Rhea, Mom, Dad, and her friends. She was yearning for her home in Patna, her family, her country.

With four consecutive classes, the day went by faster than she had expected. She attended all of them, sitting with the same people in every class, for the first time since she had been here. She didn't hear much of what they were saying at first, lost in her thoughts. She forced herself to concentrate and listen. They were halfway through the final class of the day when she checked her mobile; she had got a number of missed calls from Mitash and Enrique. And several texts.

The last text read – *I hope you are in class and not anywhere else. I need to talk to you… to see you.*

Varushka didn't respond to it straight away. She put her mobile face down in her bag and looked upward towards the lecturer. No matter how hard she tried, she could no longer concentrate on what he was saying. She didn't take her eyes off the white screen, staring at it without blinking even once until a tear escaped the corner of her eyes. She told herself it was exhaustion. She was experiencing difficulty in breathing because she had cried the whole of the previous night and had not been drinking enough water.

She quickly wiped the teardrop with the end of her scarf. She could not lose her energy when she was already getting depleted of it emotionally.

When the class ended, she didn't want to go home straight. The thought of going home transported her to the past. How perfect it was, the day when Mitash and she had their romantic pre-wedding photo-shoot. His every touch and breath to each part of her body had filled her with excitement and ecstasy.

It was still difficult to fathom, to believe what had happened in the past or what had happened yesterday.

Everything seemed to be an illusion to Varushka. She even lost faith in herself. She realized how wrong her decisions and plans had been.

To love and to be loved, is something humans crave for. But it hurts as hell when you are conned in the name of love.

Completely broken, Varushka wanted to fly away to a lonely place where she knew no one and no one knew her.

▼

"Varushka, we need to talk," Mitash said sitting next to her on the edge of her bed.

"What about?" she asked, staring at him blankly.

He looked at her, his eyes searching. He didn't look so well.

"I am sorry. I know I messed up totally. Except that, I was always truthful to you," he said, drilling his sunken eyes into her hollow brown ones. Her eyes however were missing their usual gleam.

Varushka wanted to slap him, pull his hair out in anger. But she lacked the energy to do so. She managed to remain silent for the next few seconds.

"I am ready to hear everything you have to say." She responded breaking the seemingly-never-ending silence between them.

"I never wanted to marry a girl," his voice said choked and muffled.

"Then why the hell did you marry me?" she asked.

"I didn't. It happened. It was not merely difficult, but impossible to make my parents and family understand. For them, marriage is something crucial to life, something we are born for. I agreed to marry for my family's honour…for my parents' happiness."

The words echoed inside her.

"But my parents never went with a marriage proposal to you. Then why did you choose me and ruin my life? You could have married anyone else among the proposals your family was receiving in bundles.

"Why did you send those messages on Facebook? Why did you call me on a date and propose to me? In time make me fall in love with you? Why did you convince me to choose my life with you, rejecting my promising career opportunity? I would have been happier being unmarried, Mitash," she shrieked in a breath.

"I kept rejecting so many girls, but my family left me with no option. I never intended to fool you. When I saw you first in that café in Patna, I found you so ambitious and career oriented. Someone giving preference to one's career and not to marriage or family. Someone who wanted to be something. Someone so intelligent and beautiful. I thought by marrying you, it would help both of us. It would fulfil our own agendas.

"Varushka, as promised, I will keep helping you in shaping your career. All I wanted to say to you in time is, my truth and gratitude for saving my family's honour"

"Mitash, how did you assume that for me my career was the only preference and importance in life? Yes, it was a priority, but I also wanted to get married to my dream prince after accomplishing my career goals. I wanted to be a partner in all sense to my husband. You messed up everything. I felt you were the one for me. I liked you. I fell in love with your attitude towards life, your thoughts and expectations about your life partner. I fell in love with you and you too are responsible for these feelings. The feelings of love I had always hid inside, you dug up.

"You made me realize if one gets a perfect soulmate, career and love, both can be developed together. Then I took that big chance of my life that has now turned out to be the biggest mistake. I gambled my life. And you are still saying that except one lie, you were truthful to me!"

"I agree, Varushka. I accept everything you say. But trust me, I never intended to cheat and hurt you. I thought I'd tell you the truth at the right time. I was sure you were mature and smart and would understand the situation, supporting me. I couldn't gather the courage to do so... or that right time never came."

She was listening like a mannequin.

'Why did you marry me? For my parents...' His answer echoed inside her.

Something struck her heart. "Why did I agree to marry?" she asked herself. "...for my parents?"

She married for her parents, so did he.

Self Realisation

Varushka slept a little late that night, but mostly she couldn't help thinking about what she had done and what she was doing with her life. Mitash was now sleeping in Enrique's room. She was told that Enrique had extended his stay in France due to his dad's poor health. Varushka didn't react.

Why did you marry me? For my parents.

Mitash's voice echoed inside her for the thousandth time.

"What did I marry for?" she asked herself.

"Was it really for my love for Mitash?

Love is like a deep well. You fall in, but you can never climb out. Even when you feel it's time to climb out, for some reason, there is something catching your feet, rooting it to the bottom.

Yes, I married Mitash for a reason.

Yes, Mitash has promised to support me to build my career, but why did I leave something I already had and choose an uncertainty?

I knew I had to be in the shoes of the stereotyped girl and get married. I knew this was my destiny, and life was still a gamble. Even if I had known my husband before marriage, for many years, life would have still been a gamble.

Then who is to be blamed for my destiny, Mitash, my parents, his parents or myself for being responsible for my heartbreak?

Isn't it me who let others con me, play with my feelings, emotions, my dreams and desires? Isn't it me who failed to decide what was good for me and take a stand for myself?

But what am I doing now?

Crying about my destiny? Getting angry with someone for ruining my life?"

This monologue was making Varushka crazy. She rubbed her chest, trying to ease the ache in her heart and gasped for air. It was so hard to breathe.

Suddenly the city became strange. The house with Mitash and Enrique became strange. She wanted to get out of her situation. She did not want to stay there any longer, especially with her husband who loved someone else.

Here she was in Amsterdam, one of the most wonderful and peaceful cities in the world, she had always dreamt to visit. Though now, she yearned for the smoke, aromas and noise of India.

She looked up. Only an hour ago, the blackness was absolute, but now the mist and fog were visible in slivers. Under this calming beauty, one could see the mirror of houses becoming clearer and even the branches of trees looking whiter than grey with icicles.

The morning sky glowed like a blue ocean and the sun was like a pure gold nugget in the sky. It was a perfect morning, one to be savoured instead of squandered.

A look of slow determination spread over her face. She resolved, right then and there, to return to India.

"Is there not even a single reason to chance you to stay back?" Mitash asked her when she informed him.

"For what? For whom? I find no reason to stay back," she replied in a flat emotionless tone.

"Can't we live like before? Everything was so good," he pleaded. His voice broke over the last syllable.

She didn't bother to look at him. "It is so suffocating here… now."

She booked her ticket for the next flight to Delhi and boarded it with all her belongings.

Friends' Reactions

In the present

T here was silence once Varushka was done telling her friends her story. Everyone became sober with shock listening to her story. They never thought this could be possible.

Kesha said, "You took the right decision. We are here for you."

Every day is an opportunity for a new life. Every day you stand at the tipping point of your life. On any one day, you can change the future through the way you fuel.

At Parents' Home

When Varushka arrived at Patna, her family was surprised to see her. Everyone exclaimed their curiosity in delight. Soon her 'homecoming' update was broadcasted to her neighbours, relatives and so on. Varushka's mom left no chance to not mention that her daughter who lived in a foreign country, that too in Europe, was visiting. This was followed by people meeting Varushka in the evening to quiz her about her married life in a foreign country.

Varushka looked at her dad, mom and sister. Everyone appeared so happy and excited. A daughter or a son visiting home from foreign shores is no less than a festival. The get together turns into a celebration.

She wondered what would be their reaction when they come to know that she had not come back to visit, that she had 'come back' for good. Varushka was in a dilemma, whether to tell her family about her decision or not. She did not want to transform their happiness into sorrow. She had to tell them eventually, though she wasn't sure how and when to break the news.

In Patna, everyone had only one thing to say.

"How come you are subdued?"

"Why are you not as bubbly as before?"

"You have matured so much after marriage."

Varushka had no clue how to react to this; whether to take it as a compliment or be sad about it. When she saw her room, her den, she saw that the wall behind the bed had been painted purple and a twenty-four by thirty-six-inch black and white photo from her wedding was framed on the wall. For a moment, it reminded her of the sensual and beautiful moments from her marriage. How he had bowed before her to put on the jaimala easily and thereafter how everyone had begun to hoot, teasing him for being so loyal and respectful to his wife. The bride and groom too couldn't resist laughing at that time. The memories soon washed away her little smile.

She took off the photo-frame from the wall so that it didn't remind her of him. The empty space that the photo left behind reminded her of not trying to remember him. The purpose got defeated. She began to miss the person she thought he was to her.

▼

Four weeks went past in a jiffy since she had come to Patna. Her family had asked her on several occasions about her plan, but she couldn't tell them that she had left Amsterdam for good. Varushka did sometimes feel the need to share the truth with her mom. In her darkest moments, she wondered how easy it would be to open up to her and ask for advice. However, knowing her family the way she did, she suspected more than anything else, she would get lectured about leaving her husband. For them, after a girl's marriage, the house of her husband and in-laws is her real home. Her domicile changes without any paperwork or her consent. Her mom wouldn't understand her situation, nor Mitash and Enrique's relationship. A man cares about someone, feels an emotional connection and physical attraction towards another *man*? That was simply unnatural for her family and society. Homosexuality exists, but marriage cures it. According to their logic, men who explore turn out to be caring and intimate husbands.

Varushka faced the lowest of lows of her life. The experience completely transformed the way she looked at love and life. The rose-tinted glasses were finally off. She could see her marriage with Mitash as her family's desperation to get her married to a good looking, high-earning NRI boy.

She looked through the recent posts of her friends on Facebook and those led her to their Instagram feeds. Most of the pictures posted were of outing with colleagues, vacations on beaches and hills, weekend evenings in pubs, conferences and meetings across the globe. Few of her seniors shared pics from their engagements, marriages or announcing their pregnancies. Some were of her elder cousins enjoying moments with their children and family. In short, everyone seemed Happily Employed, Happily Married. She tried to remember when she had celebrated her life, and found it was around three months ago.

She looked in the mirror. She was disgusted by what she saw. She looked at herself differently. A failure in life! She failed in making her career. She failed in her marriage. She failed in convincing her family and herself about her dreams and desires. She failed in finding her own identity.

Yes, she too was married happily, but couldn't live with its façade any longer.

Varushka shook herself out of it before the thoughts could sink her deeper into sadness. During the day, mostly, she could pretend nothing was wrong and survive without crying even once. She was fine when she was watching a movie, but a movie full of romance made her feel worse. Her daily assignments were to keep herself occupied every second of every day. She watched a lot of TV shows and movies on her laptop. She slept when she couldn't find anything to keep her mind away from thinking about Mitash.

Whenever she would see a guy with a dimple, her thoughts would travel back to him. Whenever she would see someone painting, her thoughts would travel back to him. Whenever she saw his favourite food, her thoughts would travel back to him. Whenever she saw his favourite colour, her thoughts would travel back to him. Whenever she listened to his favourite music, her thoughts would travel back to him. Whenever she would get a whiff of the fragrance of his perfume, her thoughts would travel back to him. Whenever she would see a kissing scene in a movie, her thoughts would travel back to him.

In fact, whenever she saw a betrayal scene, her thoughts would travel back to him.

Mitash had betrayed her. Her feelings and love for him were real. She had loved Mitash truly, and that was something stopping her to unveil his dual life in front of everyone. She now knew what she had with Mitash was different.

She missed his chuckling, endless chats with him, cooking together and his care for her besides his mentoring and motivating her dreams and goals.

He had planned trips to fulfil her wish list. He planned the skydiving session for Varushka, even when he was scared of heights himself. He dived into the sea, even when he didn't like water, to ensure that she was not alone and was safe.

"How can a person pretend to be so good to someone?" she asked herself. "Or maybe he was not pretending all the way at all. What would he get out of pretending to be nice to her, liking and loving towards her? His motto of getting married and massaging over his parent's societal ego was already over. Maybe she had built it up, turned it into something that wasn't there."

The next moment, her heart revolted against that idea. No! No! That cannot be.

"What if his care for her was true? Everything he did for her, to keep her happy, to support her achieving her dream surely couldn't be fake. Her heart was not ready to accept that everything had been fake.

While being with him, she never for a second doubted that it wasn't true love or they weren't supposed to be together. There was no barrier strong enough to separate them from each other completely. She knew and felt it too.

"But then, why did I leave him and fly back to India and am now in my parents' home? Mitash can't love me the way I deserve and desire. He loves Enrique, a man!" her mind alarmed her heart.

Varushka's eyes filled up with tears. She let them flow freely into her hair.

"But why can't he?" her heart argued.

"If he can and he does, will you be going back to him again? To restart a family of husband-wife and husband's boyfriend?

Enrique is his first love and he still loves him," her mind screamed.

"Leave me alone. I don't know where my life is taking me. What I am living for?" Her heart was tired of arguing. She lay on her bed, closing her tear-filled eyes.

▼

She served herself some roasted parched rice and was filling up her bowl with *ghughni* when her mom spoke. "What's going on, Varushka?"

"What do you mean?" Varushka asked evenly.

"Papa and I are worried about you. You seems so changed since you have come home. You look so sick these days. You're not showing interest in anything. You don't talk much to us. You didn't tell us about your vacation plan. Have you already booked your return ticket?"

"Nope! I am not going."

"What do you mean?"

"I can't go back."

"Can't go back! What are you saying? Is there something bothering you? Is there any issue with your visa?" her mom asked.

"Visa is fine. I have just come back for good."

"But why? You are married. Your husband lives there, your life and future is there. How can you simply leave him alone and come? Did you fight with Mitash?" her dad asked.

Varushka looked at her parents in exasperation.

"Darling, these silly fights keep happening between couples. It takes time to understand each other. Be comfortable and adjust with each other. There can be no reason to leave your house like this," her mom tried to convince her.

"I am not a child to behave in a silly way. If it would have been so simple a reason, I would have figured it out. I know it's not as easy as it sounds to leave everything and decide to return to one's *maikey*."

"Then at least tell us what's the matter? What's going on? We will talk to Mitash regarding this. We will also talk to his family." Her dad was becoming restless.

She had always given an excuse to avoid connecting her parents with Mitash and his family. She used to make blank calls and say they were busy to have a long conversation.

Varushka was in a dilemma whether to tell her family about Mitash's sexuality or not. Whether they would be able to handle it in the right way? She did not want this to spread to all those known to her family and from them to those whom she didn't know at all. However, Mitash had lied to her. On the flip side, he was so caring and loving all the way. She did not want to make it a family issue and a topic for malicious gossip for relatives and the society. It would never make her life easy. She simply wanted to come out of this marriage and move on.

"We have already talked about this. Nothing can be changed now. I am not going back at all."

"Then what do you want to do? What's going on in your mind, girl?"

"Divorce!" she replied in a single word without moving her eyes from her cutlery.

"Do you know what you are blabbering?"

"I want to walk out of this marriage," she elaborated.

The term 'divorce' is considered even worse than death. The celebration of her visit turned into mourning all of a sudden.

"Marriage isn't a child's game that whenever you want, get married and when you don't want it, walk out of it. If there is any problem, it can be solved."

"Even tearing my job offer letter was not a game. I studied so many years to get that. But you people made me walk out of my dream, my goal, my ambition, dignity…"

"…so you want to take revenge?" her Dad interjected. "We married you to Mitash with your consent. You can't deny it."

"And you know very well how and what you did to make me choose the life I didn't want then. My marriage was your only dream, your last responsibility as my parents towards me."

She paused and said sarcastically, "…Oh yes! So now you might be feeling burdened with that responsibility once again?"

"Shut up, Varushka! Have you gone mad? What has happened to you that you are talking like this to us, your parents? You know how much we love you. How could you even say that? We gave you all the freedom, education…"

"Happy? If you would have allowed me to pursue my dream without these distractions, I would have been really happy… been alive and living happily."

"Stop making such a fuss, Varushka. You could fulfil all your dreams even after you got married. Tell me, weren't you very happy since the last time we spoke to you before your surprise visit to Patna?"

Varushka didn't reply and kept playing with the spoon.

"Okay. Why did you want to work? To earn money, to go on holidays abroad, and to have a luxurious life. You are already enjoying these and even more. You only told us that Mitash got you enrolled in a course there to upgrade your knowledge before you apply for a job there. You'd be working soon. Then what's the problem?"

"And why did I get married? To enjoy these luxuries?"

Everyone was staring at her with no idea what was happening with her.

Dad interjected.

"We did not get you married to bring trouble in your life. Enough Varushka, will you tell us what's wrong? Until you tell us, how will we be in a position to understand and…"

Varushka could not hold her emotional distress anymore and broke down. "My marriage was a big lie, mom. It ruined my life. I gave up my dream, my plan for life for this marriage, which was never meant to be… he betrayed me." She hid her face with her palms, sobbing uncontrollably.

It was a big shock for her parents to hear the word 'betrayed'.

"Oh god! That's why I was never in favour of marrying my daughter to an NRI. They keep a mistress or get married to a white girl and then prove themselves as 'so-called cultured', while they have an arranged marriage to an innocent trusting god-fearing Indian girl," said her mother.

Varushka wanted to yell, 'Yes! He has an extramarital affair, and that too with *a man*. I can't compromise *ever*. Actually, no one should ever have to.' But she couldn't tell them about Mitash's reality.

When her parents didn't stop for the next whole minute with their ill-informed analysis, Varushka left the meal unfinished and locked herself in her room which now belonged to Rhea. People she loved needed to stop assuming. They needed to listen and help her reach a solution rather than play certified marriage counsellers, pointing to areas of her ignorance, which was not true.

The fact was she loved Mitash too.

She just couldn't stop crying. She felt that there was something else, something big that had been taken away from her. She had been confident as a child and a certain amount of self worth she always tended to have until she felt someone snatch it away from her. She had lost all her essence of self-esteem when Mitash's reality revealed itself to her. She had suddenly lost her purpose, her dream, her ambition and her desire to do something, be something.

There was a knock on her door. Varushka sniffed and wiped her tears on her pillow. She sat on her bed and looked for something to check her reflection. She didn't want her family seeing her crying. She didn't want to hurt them more than she had just done.

She took a few seconds to compose herself before opening the door. It was Rhea. Varushka turned around and sat down on her bed. Rhea turned on the light and closed the door before sitting next to her. She didn't say anything.

Rhea couldn't handle the silence. "Di, I know you must not have taken this decision without thinking a lot or giving it one more chance. I am also sure there must be a big reason, else you would not have given up so easily. However, I am not able to understand what happened so suddenly? Just until last week you were so happy. I had seen that over the video calls. What has happened in a week that you've decided to divorce Mitash Jiju?"

"You won't understand Rhea. You are not married yet." Varushka sniffed.

"I will understand or not, that comes later. First, you try to make me understand," Rhea tried to convince her sister to speak the truth.

Varushka was playing with words in her mind. She wasn't sure what to tell Rhea or how to say it.

"I don't have any idea whether you would understand these things about life or believe it. I was not ready to get married at that point. I had a great job opportunity that could have led me to USA after a year. You know very well how Mom and Dad emotionally blackmailed me. They even called Bua to convince me. Besides, you also got into their influence, which forced me a lot to agree to the match. I seriously hate Manisha Maasi. She manipulated Mom a lot, resulting in our family dramas.

"It was not that I was trying to be a so-called feminist, running away from marriage. I only needed time to explore and understand life on my own. There is a life outside home, this city and this whole so-called society. I am a normal girl who had dreamt of her prince charming, marriage, honeymoon and kids too. I know all this seems so unreal that I had them in my wish list, because all the time I kept advocating for girl's education, career, decision and self-dependency. It's true, these were there as well. For me, a girl is also a human being and has the right to explore and stand for her own dignity and that could make her a happy wife and later a happy mother. The only thing I wanted was to step forward in a sequence of my path to achieving it.

"However, my plan for my life was out of our family's thoughts. Mitash was right. For parents, the ultimate responsibility is to get their child married. It is the solution to all of life's problems. It is like this concept being similar to doctors with fake degrees who consider that the same medicine can cure all ailments."

Rhea was listening patiently.

Varushka continued. "So after thinking a lot, considering all the love I was given and sacrifices made by our parents which were verbalized as expense investment sheets, I accepted and convinced myself to marry Mitash. I agree that it was not a coerced decision to marry Mitash. Somehow it appeared I couldn't meet anyone better than him, then.

"It was the first time I let my heart open up for someone, let myself fall for someone, felt those special moments. I accepted him, liked him, married him and loved him. Everything was going well. It was like a fairytale life as if a film was scripted for me with everything happening perfectly. We ate and drank together, sang together, danced together, talked happily – life was so much fun. He helped me achieve every bit of happiness. Even Enrique was a big support. Everything was so perfect. However, no movie, no story can exist without a tragedy. Then how could I expect it from my life!

"I was deeply in love with Mitash. I surrendered my life, my destiny to him. Then the most bitter truth opened up in my life. I found Mitash's personal diary which he had never mentioned about. I came to know that Mitash is not a normal conventional man…"

Varushka paused and took a deep breath.

"What do you mean by not normal? Is he a psycho? Did he harm you?" Rhea broke the silence.

"If he had been a psycho, there would have been a possibility to compromise, Rhea," she spoke with a broken heart.

"The curiosity of knowing what he feels about me, and hadn't shared with me yet made me turn the pages of his diary. I kept turning the pages randomly forwards and backwards to know his feelings during the initial days of our meeting and then there was the most heartbreaking moment for me. The secret that shattered me from inside…" she said, choking on her words.

"What was written there?" Rhea's heartbeat had also increased.

"Enrique and Mitash were always in a relationship and in love with each other…"

"*What?*" Rhea screamed as quietly as possible. "You mean he is gay? Are you serious? How did you come to know?"

"He confessed!"

"Unbelievable!" It was something unbelievable for Rhea. It seemed so unreal. She had not seen or met any homosexual or bisexual person in her life, nor had she ever heard about anyone, apart from movies, books and the news.

"For a week I was expecting him to tell me it was just a prank. I had never imagined that such an incident could happen to me."

"But Di, when did you come to know about it? Why the hell did you not utter a word about this to us? If he is gay, why did he send you the marriage proposal and marry you?" Rhea asked again.

Varushka's lips trembled. "Maybe the same reason I married him…"

She wiped off her tears with the back of her hand and said, "You know, Rhea, when someone says that he is marrying for the sake of his parents or because his family wants him to get married, beware! It's a big big trap. An *alarm* for you! Most of the time, the decision of getting married for one's parents' happiness hides an ugly truth behind and that could destroy you from the inside."

The thought was too sad and complicated for Rhea to grasp and comprehend immediately. When Rhea looked at her sister, she noticed how much she had changed in a short time. She was no longer the girl she used to be. Her zeal and zest were lost somewhere. Her confidence, her self-esteem and love had been shaken off. After all, her decision had gone so wrong. When Varushka planned her life and career forward, her current circumstances brought her back to square one.

Rhea hugged Varushka. It gave some relief to Varushka after a long time.

"Di, does Jiju know that you want to divorce him? I mean Mitash… I mean Mitash Jiju," she stumbled saying.

"Even I hadn't realized that I want to give him a divorce until I told Mom and Dad…"

"Hmm… but do you really think it would be as easy to actually get the divorce as against just wishing for it? What if he denies it?"

"I have no idea…"

"Leave him or his family. I am sure Mom will call all her 'army members' to convince you to surrender this idea. And what if you got the divorce? People here will definitely make your life hell. I wish I was working in some other city. I would have taken care of you, away from all these people."

Varushka smiled hearing her sister's words of concern.

"Okay, let's not think too much now. It's already too late in the night – almost quarter past two. One of my friend's brother is a lawyer. I am sure he could be of some help. Or might help with some suggestion. I'll contact her tomorrow," Rhea said holding her sister who really needed the warm hug to heal a bit.

▼

"So, is your husband also ready for a divorce?" Ritvik Singh, the lawyer, asked Varushka. He was tall and lean. His hazel-coloured eyes and thick unruly hair made him look like a model rather than a lawyer. His personality could have fetched him quite a lot of offers to walk the ramp rather than to go to a court-room, Varushka wondered in amazement. However, in his Armani suit over his off-white shirt matched with a charcoal small triangle pattern tie and swanky interiors of his office, displayed the number of rich, affluent clients he had profited from.

"Umm, I have no idea. But he won't have any other option," Varushka explained.

"So, how long have you both been separated?" he asked.

"Not officially separated yet. I left his home and came to India a month back," she replied.

"Isn't it common for Indian married women to stay with their parents for a one month vacation? See Varushka, it's not that easy to get a divorce without mutual consent. Settling a divorce isn't as easy as they show in the movies or daily soaps. Do you have any grounds? I mean, any infidelity in your marriage? Or does your husband mentally, physically torture and abuse you?"

"He is gay!" she said starkly, making Ritvik look at her like she was talking about an alien.

Ritvik cleared his throat. "Do you know what you are saying? I have already told you that it's not a movie. We are dealing with real life."

"So, am I saying something so unreal?" she asked.

"Cool down, Varushka." Ritvik offered her a glass of water. "I agree that you are not saying so unreal a thing, but still it is not so common around us. This case sounds interesting. But how do you know?"

"He confessed."

"Before marriage?"

"No, after a few months of marriage, as I found this truth from somewhere."

"Cool! So it means your marriage has not been consummated? Means, you guys did not ever have sex? The non-consummation of a marriage would render the marriage voidable. Once the marriage itself is a voidable marriage, there is no question of a divorce," he explained.

Ritvik's excitement couldn't excite Varushka. "Aren't you happy to know how easily this case could be solved?" Ritvik was surprised to see Varushka's expressionless face.

Varushka hesitated.

"We had sex... if it is called sex! I am still a virgin," she replied looking at Ritvik, waiting for his reaction.

"Have you gone crazy or are you trying to fool me?" he asked, letting the annoyance show. "You said your husband is gay, means he sexually indulges with men, and now you are saying that he had sex with you once, but you are a virgin!"

"Can't you do anything?" Varushka resorted to pleading.

"Well Varushka, many things can be done. But, if you want a correct treatment or a correct legal solution, you need not hide anything from a doctor or a lawyer. I am sure you must be well aware of this fact. I can't help you until I understand your case thoroughly. So can we go ahead with the details, please?"

Varushka narrated the story for the second time in the last twenty hours.

"If you want to give Mitash a divorce on the grounds of him being gay and keeping his truth hidden from you before marriage, will he or his family accept this in court? Or how will

you prove it? You both had a form of intercourse and this may
or may not be easily proven through a medical test. As you say
you are still a virgin and you two were involved in an act, this
again can point many questions at you. You are mature enough
to understand that even you will be putting your family and your
reputation at stake."

"Can't I get a divorce?"

"If you can prove any kind of infidelity in your marriage or
something like he is already married to someone else, harassed
or abused you physically or mentally or something like that... or
if he agrees to sign the divorce papers," Ritvik suggested. "Have
you been to any counsellor?"

"No!" she replied.

"And is your family ready for this?"

Varushka denied it, answering with her silence.

"Do they know you are talking about divorce and visiting a
lawyer?" Ritvik looked at her and was horrified reading her face,
trying to understand what was going on in her mind.

"I just told them last night, at dinner, that I want to walk out
of my marriage."

"How could you keep this from your family for so long?"
Ritvik looked upset at hearing about her behaviour.

"So that I don't have anyone else to blame for this decision
unlike my decision to get married. I married as they wanted to
get me married off. But after that, it was I who agreed to get
married and now I am responsible for going through this painful
period. Now I decided I don't want to be in this trap anymore."

"Varushka, I know you are beautiful, highly qualified and
also, a legal adult. You have the full right to take any decision
you want. However, what if things don't go as you want? What if

your family doesn't support this decision? I have seen many such cases. Divorce cases like yours are most of the time very long and expensive. How will you be able to support the expenses of the case when you do not make your own living? I will suggest that you first discuss an amicable divorce with your husband so that he agrees to sign the divorce papers and then talk to your parents too. Most importantly, try to get a job so that no one can manipulate and pressurize you from divorcing. Hope you get my point."

Varushka thanked him and stood up to leave.

The Next Step

"What do you really really want?" Varushka heard a voice in her head as she drove back home.

"A happy and peaceful life," her heart replied.

"And how would you get that?" her inner voice asked. "You left everything in between. You left your dream job to get married. You want to walk out of your marriage and then the studies there. This could have landed you a big job, however you have left it to get divorced. Is your life meant to revolve around only these two things?"

"I don't know," she answered.

"Then who else will know?" her inner voice screamed out loud.

"Then what should I do?" she whined. "Salvage my marriage? Keep everyone happy?"

"Yes, if it really makes *everyone* happy," the inner voice conquered in reply.

"Yes, I was happy until I figured out the big lie. Even then, was Mitash happy, or what about Enrique, who was bravely sharing his love with someone else?" Varushka thought. "I should have made the extra effort to avoid this marriage in the first place. Hurting my parents a little then would have been easier on them than knowing that I am going to divorce Mitash now. It is like a double whammy pain – my failed marriage and they are the reason for it, at least for them."

"Should I really try to save my marriage if it can help them be peaceful at their age?" her mind asked.

"But what is there for me in this marriage? Is a marriage with love, without making love? Can a woman settle for it?" her heart questioned.

"Am I the only one in this situation?" her inner voice asked.

Varushka was getting crazy with so many questions flooding her mind.

She parked the car in the parking lot in front of her house.

"Hey. You're home. How was the meeting?" Taking her eyes off her WhatsApp messages, Rhea waved at Varushka as she entered the room.

"Not too bad, actually," Varushka said throwing her sling bag on the couch and collapsed on her bed. She was so exhausted and restless. She typed 'Gay Men Marrying Straight Women' in Google search.

She was surprised to see several threads appearing in results. Breathing steadily, she focused her mind. She began opening all the links one by one. Few were connected to many other pages and threads as well. After reading for an hour, she was assured that she was not alone in such a situation. Not only in India, but also in some other parts of the world, there were many gay men who shared their experiences of how they entered into wedlock hiding their sexuality to please their family and society. However, when the truth was revealed to the women, the marriages broke down.

Many women, in fact, Indian women had shared their stories of how shocked, shattered and heartbroken they were when they discovered their husbands had played with their emotions and were satisfying their sexual needs outside the marriage with other men.

She found one news article[1] on how a girl ended her life when she wasn't able to walk out of the marriage with her gay husband. Few of such couples have had kids as well.

One of the reports said, "Approximately 85 per cent of these mixed-orientation couples eventually do separate, while the remaining 15 per cent continue their marriage, usually with some mutually devised alternative contract[2]."

After three hours of browsing, Varushka had investigated enough information that gave her some sort of relief after a long time. She saw a trace of light. She felt as if she had found a way out of the absolute darkness. If there is a way in, there is a way out. It is just a matter of thinking clearly until you find it.

"Excellent! So, what have you planned next?" Rhea asked Varushka, handing over the printed copies of the researched information.

"To discuss this with Mitash so that we dissolve our marriage without making it any more complicated and search for a job as well," Varushka replied with sparkling eyes. Rhea was delighted to see her sister in a positive mood for the first time since she had come back from Amsterdam.

1. https://www.telegraphindia.com/1150426/jsp/7days/story_16660.jsp
2. https://goodmenproject.com/marriage-2/women-partly-blame-staying-married-gayman-dg/

"Di, why don't you call Technesight and ask them if you can still join them? Just a thought. Just a try," Rhea suggested.

"Darn! I already tore their offer letter," Varushka said with disappointment.

Rhea sniffed. "Uff Di. Are you still in the 90s era? You must have some mail from them as well. Check your previous mails. Give it a try."

"Oh, yes. You have become. Let me check," Varushka said kissing Rhea.

"Don't forget to check your Junk and other Spam folders. You never know, there might be some important mail you may need," Rhea reminded her before leaving the room.

In her bed, Varushka drafted a mail to the company that had given her a job offer during her campus selection, which she never joined, asking them if there was still any possibility for them to allow her to join them. She attached all the previous references as well with a fabricated 'medical emergency' as the reason for not being able to join them, then. She proofread the email and sent it. A sense of positivity filled her insides.

She opened the folder of her blocked emails. She had received almost forty 'sorry' emails from Mitash and few were from Enrique too, that she had never read or replied to. One by one, she opened all of Mitash's mails. Few she read thoroughly and few she simply glanced through. She, however, didn't open any of the emails sent from Enrique.

She opened the last email of Mitash which she had received that morning. Earlier she was thinking that Mitash had not even tried to contact her after she had left Amsterdam. She was somewhat overwhelmed seeing his messages, confessing his mistake of hiding the fact, requesting her to come back and

pleading not to tell anything to anyone as it was going to turn out
to be a big big family mess.

The warm corner in her heart for Mitash was alive again.
However, she couldn't agree that how not telling anyone wouldn't
make a mess in her life.

Varushka decided to finally write to Mitash and offer him a
deal.

Mitash

*I really don't know how you felt all this time, since I
left your house. It took me almost a month and a half
to understand what exactly was happening and what I
want and should do now to protect my interests.*

*I totally understand how you wished to hide the fact
of your true self as thousands and thousands of other gay
men are doing – hiding the truth of their sexuality and
marrying to massage the social status of their family,
while some of them even brought babies into this world
to be socially acceptable.*

*Mitash, my love for you was true. Your love for
Enrique is true, your feelings as a best friend for me may
be true. However, this relationship turned out to be a lie.
I can't stand by it. I can't be party to your equation. It
is unacceptable for me to live with my husband and his
love, his boyfriend.*

I want a divorce from you.

*Let's make another deal. You sign the divorce papers
and I will not tell anyone why we separated.*

Varushka

Sanchit's Engagement

"Get ready on time. Don't be late, we will be leaving by nine," her mom announced for the fourth time, ensuring everyone woke up and started getting ready. It was Rhea and Varushka's cousin Sanchit's engagement in the afternoon. Her mom wanted to be there early to meet other family members and get the details of the wedding. Sanchit was Varushka's elder uncle's son, a software developer in Infosys, Pune. His parents had fixed his marriage with a journalist, Vinita, from Patna who recently got placed in a Mumbai-based media house after completing her studies from Symbiosis Pune.

"Get ready properly and look like a happily married woman," her Mom instructed Varushka as she came out after her bath, wrapping a blue towel around her hair.

"What's this looking like a happily married woman? How does makeup and my dressing make a difference about being married or not? Earlier I used to wear a lehnga, suit or saree for family functions like this and so did you. Do I have to wear a saree with a label that reads 'I am happily married'?" Varushka said exasperated, throwing her arms in the air.

"Also put a bindi, precisely red, wear dark lipstick, properly visible sindoor, new toe rings and heavy jewellery with bangles. You are going to be part of the family function for the first time after your marriage, so wear your *dholna* too. Please don't speak a single word about you wanting to divorce or look miserable. Hope you get my point. I don't want anyone to make any negative comments about you or your marriage," instructed Varushka's mom.

Varushka refused to debate with her mom any further. She was anxiously waiting for a reply from Mitash and also Technesight. She wanted to be free to plan ahead. She looked at Rhea who was grinning at her while eating her breakfast. Varushka soon joined her for breakfast.

"What are we going to do reaching there so soon? I don't want any encounter with any of our aunts or uncles besides getting bombarded by their endless queries about my personal, social and professional life," Varushka whispered.

"Same pinch. Do we have any choice?" Rhea added.

"Hold on! What if we make a deal with Mom?" Varushka said.

"I would really appreciate it if you want to give a try," Rhea replied with a wicked smile.

"Mom, you want me to get ready with a happily married look, correct?" Varushka questioned.

"Yes, hope you understand what I mean by that," her mom answered, giving her a strange wondering look.

"Cool! I need to buy a few things from the nearby mall. A blouse for the most beautiful and stunning saree, which also needs a small repair and that I can get done after 11 a.m. today. So is it fine if Rhea and I reach the venue by 1 p.m. as the engagement is not going to start before 2 p.m." In this way Varushka proposed her plan of staying back at home longer.

Her mom pondered over the thought for a few seconds in silence. "Okay, it sounds good to me. Hope you won't disappoint your dad and me. And one more thing, don't try to make an excuse for not appearing at the event."

"Done! I would never do that."

Varushka was happy that she had peacefully convinced her mom.

▼

"Do you want to rehearse your moves? We still have some time," Rhea asked while searching for matching accessories for her grey lehnga.

"What's that about?" Varushka asked.

"Aunty was telling me that they have some dance schedule for the family members," Rhea explained.

"Absolutely not! I am really not interested in anything like that. Hey, should we buy some gifts for the soon to be engaged couple?" Varushka enquired. "Sanchit Bhaiya always sends gifts for us."

"I like this idea, but do we have enough time to go, buy gifts, come home to get ready and then go for the engagement?" Rhea asked.

"How about this? Let's get ready and go to the nearby mall, buy their gift and directly reach the venue," Varushka proposed to Rhea.

"Sounds good to me," Rhea smirked.

Defeating the unwritten law that women take hours to get ready, the two sisters were ready in the next thirty minutes.

"Wow Di! You look more ravishing than you did on your own engagement day. Is this the 'being married' effect or 'soon to be divorced' effect?" Rhea chuckled. "Forget the others, Mom is definitely going to lose her mind with beaming pride seeing you in this traditionally voguish avatar," she added.

Quite familiar with her way around Patna, Varushka drove directly to the mall near the engagement venue. Parking the car outside, Varushka stepped out in her sequin-studded peach crepe saree paired with a beautiful net embroidered blouse matched with chandelier earrings, and a full set of bangles. A round shaped big tika was perfectly placed between the centre of her curly locks waving to her waist, the *dholna-sindoor-bindi* all intact as per her mom's instructions. Rhea was in her grey lehnga paired with oxidized silver jewellery. In the mid-afternoon sun, passersby stopped to take a quick glance at the beautiful sisters.

Certainly, they felt like complete showstoppers at the mall. However, without caring for those staring eyes around them, they walked around the mall in search of the best possible gift for the couple. After a long brainstorming session, the sister duo ended up buying a watch for Sanchit Bhaiya, as he had a big-time craze for watches, and an enchanting perfume for their soon-to-be bhabhi.

"Wow, what is he doing here?" Rhea said patting Varushka's shoulder who was busy putting the gifts in the back seat of the car.

"Who are you talking about?" Varushka asked without looking at her.

"Sanchit Bhaiya," she replied.

Sanchit was in his car with a girl, in the parking area, at some distance from Varushka's car.

"And who is this girl? His fiancée?" Varushka and Rhea exchanged a look with many more questions popping in their heads.

Sanchit got a jolt seeing his cousins there.

"Are you not supposed to be at your engagement or a salon?" Varushka asked, raising one eyebrow.

He froze for a moment turning ashen with guilt.

"Hey, what are you girls doing here?" Sanchit said breaking the silence, pretending to sound normal.

"Came to buy you a gift and also for…" Rhea said without completing her sentence.

"I could sense something not going well. Can we help you in any way?" Varushka questioned catching Sanchit's pale face. "And who is she?" she asked pointing towards the girl next to him with the red and swollen puffed eyes.

"There is nothing going on. You both carry on. I will see you in some time," Sanchit replied, trying hard to fake a weak smile.

"Bhaiya!! Are you going to tell us what's going on or you want us to call home about this? We sisters can help you," Rhea gave a naughty smile.

Sanchit looked at the third girl present, closed his eyes, three deep breaths, thrice, and said, "This is Monica, my girlfriend, for eight years."

"What! Are you kidding?" Varushka said, shocked.

"No, I am not," he responded sadly.

"Could you please explain to me in detail?" Varushka said seriously, folding her arms across her chest.

"Okay listen. We've known each other for the last ten years, since we were preparing for our engineering entrance, after our tenth board exams. We were in the same coaching institute, same batch, same class. After that, we both got admission into NIT, Warangal. She studied Electricals, and I did my Bachelors in Computer Science. After the second year, we both moved in together, outside the hostel in a rented apartment.

"You mean live in?" Rhea interrupted with her naughty smile.

"Hmm. She got a job in Bangalore, I moved to Hyderabad. We got placed through our college, so we didn't want to take the risk of losing our opportunities. The distance from Hyderabad to Bangalore is not much, so we managed to see each other over weekends or other holidays. After few months into my job, I told my parents about Monica. Her parents were already pressurising her for marriage. Somehow, her family agreed after one year. However, my parents have stayed rigid, showing no intention of allowing me to marry Monica."

"God! What's wrong with them? She looks so beautiful. She is educated, working and earning as much as you. I am sure she is a good hearted woman that you fell for. Then why do they not like her?" Varushka asked.

"She belongs to a different and lower caste than ours, according to mom and dad," Sanchit replied. "If they would have agreed, how would they have been able to sell me off for twenty-five lakhs? They managed that by arranging my marriage to Vinita."

"Quite reasonable," Varushka remarked.

"But what are you both up to?" asked Rhea getting them back to the present.

"I will be absolutely fine if you consider me wrong. However, you won't understand what I have gone through while trying to convince my parents to accept Monica. I was left with the choice to choose either them or Monica. How can I leave them? They brought me into this world, struggled to give everything to me, made me the successful engineer I am today. So defeated, I decided to go ahead with their choice for their happiness," Sanchit explained.

The last sentence was a deja vu for Varushka. "For parents…" she repeated in a muffled voice looking at the other side blankly, with tears welling up in her eyes.

"So what are you doing here with the love you decided not to choose for your life?" Rhea asked.

"I haven't finished saying everything yet. It became clear to me that nothing can move them. In fact, many times I rejected wedding proposals, and a few times I requested the girls to do the same for me. It was never-ending, for the last three years. I wanted to put a stop to all this. When I met Vinita, I told her everything. Surprisingly, she was also going through the same situation and wanted to ask me a favour to say 'no' to her family. Her family did not agree to her marrying her Tamil boyfriend.

"Suddenly, a thought clicked in her head at that moment. She too was trying to convince her family for the last few years, unfortunately, in vain. Hence, we made a deal. We decide to get engaged. Then, let our families cherish their share of moments. We get married and then within a few months get divorced by mutual consent. Thereafter, we are free and will get married to our true loves respectively," Sanchit revealed his plan.

An awkward silence followed for nearly a minute.

"Pheww… and Monica and Vinita's boyfriend also agreed? Don't you think you guys are going to mess up everything? Marriage is not a game, Bhaiya. I was expecting you to be more mature," Varushka snapped back, disappointed.

"Varushka, it is not like it was easy for me. For anyone else either. What else could we have done? Do you have any alternative?"

"It is going to be more complicated later. Trust me. Your family will be more hurt knowing that you are going for a divorce than now, knowing you want to marry one of your choices and not remain married to the one they arranged for you."

Sanchit was listening quietly. "What if Vinita and you change your mind after marriage?" Varushka questioned giving a warning look at Monica.

The changed expression of Monica's face and her tear-filled eyes were clearly indicating that Varushka had succeeded in her intention of a situation of probability in favour of Monica.

"Varushka is correct. If we are not able to make it happen today, there is no guarantee that we will achieve our goal later. Our parents will always be there," Monica said in a sad tone, looking at Sanchit with her wet eyes. "I am not letting you marry Vinita. I am calling Krishna Subramanian now," she protested.

A sarcastic smile floated on Varushka's face. "Who is he now?" she enquired.

"Vinita's boyfriend," Sanchit replied.

Monica called Krishna and added Vinita on the conference call with the speaker on so that Sanchit too could join the discussion. For another twenty minutes, a heated discussion was on among the four lovers, reworking their fixed plan which was now a mess.

Just then, Rhea received a call from her mom. "Hey, where are you girls? Something has gone wrong here. Sanchit is missing and even his mobile is not reachable. Even Vinita has locked herself in a room. She's not talking or letting anyone inside.

If you both are still at home, stay there. I will call you later to inform whether to come or not," her mom said.

"We are already on the way, Mom. Will be reaching very soon. Tell Badi Mom, everything is going to be alright, not to worry much about Bhaiya," Rhea consoled her.

"Everyone is very tense about you. Your mobile is switched off and you being the to-be-groom is not at the event as yet," Rhea explained.

"I am not able to understand what we should do now?" Sanchit asked everyone.

"I haven't told anyone yet, but it's the urge of time that I need to break this news. Because of a stupid decision, same as yours, I am on the verge of getting divorced. You guys have no idea what I am going through or how my parents are responding. Now I wish, my soon to be ex-husband would have had the courage to raise his voice then," Varushka's voice broke and drops of tears trickled down her cheeks.

"Are you kidding me?" Sanchit asked. He felt a jolt.

Everyone was silent for a few seconds.

"Can I talk to KS and Vinita once?" Varushka asked almost snatching the phone.

She turned on the handset mode, going a little far from them. She returned after speaking to KS and Vinita for ten minutes.

"What about today's function, I mean engagement? Our families, relatives and friends are waiting there," Sanchit enquired.

"Best things never come without hardship. Nothing is free. It will always cost you," Varushka replied.

"What does it mean? I mean, right now?" Sanchit asked.

"Give me your credit card and go to the venue. Talk with your family. Rhea and I will see you in some time," Varushka ordered.

"What are you up to?" Sanchit enquired.

"Do you want to marry Monica or not?" she retorted.

"Of course!" he replied with a new zest and enthusiasm.

"Then do as I say," she commanded.

▼

Everyone was hopping mad when Sanchit, in his sky blue jeans and a black tee, and Vinita, in her golden lehnga, without any jewellery, stepped into the function hall. The uncles and aunties gathered in the banquet hall tch-tched. Sanchit's mom placed one of her hands on her chest and ran towards him.

"Where were you? Why was your phone off? We were so scared!" she screamed in her shrill voice.

"Why did you lock yourself in that room for so long?" Vinita's mom had reached her by then too.

Sanchit cleared his throat. "We want to speak to all of you together," Sanchit said addressing Vinita's and his parents.

"Okay," Sanchit's dad said and everyone nodded. "We are listening."

Vinita looked at Sanchit and then turned to her mom and dad, "You know I wanted to marry Krishna and was trying to convince you both since the last three years."

Her father grimaced in embarrassment saying, "Yes!"

"I also failed to make you change your mind, since so many years," Sanchit said to his parents, "regarding my love for Monica."

The crease between the eyebrows of his dad appeared as his nose wrinkled as he admitted sheepishly. "Yes!"

Both families scanned each other awkwardly as the secrets tumbled out.

"But you both agreed to marry each other. What's the point of this now?" Vinita's mom interrupted.

"We are sorry you are about to be embarrassed before your guests," Sanchit replied.

Everyone there exchanged a mournful, nervous looks. An ominous bell had already rung in their heads.

"We can't do this now. We can't get married and we hope you will forgive us," Vinita added.

"This is surely some kind of a cosmic joke," someone commented between the hu-haahs.

"Why? What happened all of a sudden?" Varushka's father asked looking at Sanchit and Vinita, in support of his brother, Sanchit's father, who seemed to be building up towards an anxiety attack.

"Because they were never ready for that," Varushka stepped up from behind with Rhea. "They were executing Plan B."

Everyone gazed at her and gawked at her in surprise.

"Plan B?" they repeated.

Sanchit thought for a while, then admitted. "Yes, Plan B. Getting engaged, then married and after some time, getting a divorce."

Chaos of murmurs filled the venue. A collective tch-tch swept across the family, relatives and the family friends at the mention of the 'D' word. "How could you do this? How could you bring such shame upon us?" the drama began. "If you both didn't want to marry, why did you agree to it first?" Varushka's dad stepped in.

Vinita shuffled her feet and Sanchit breathed deeply, closing his eyes. Varushka and Rhea looked at each other. Varushka knew she had to whip up the 'youngsters-teaching-the-elders' speeches to get them to see the light.

"To make their families happy as they failed to convince them to marry Monica and Krishna, respectively," Varushka replied, then continued. "We understand how important the marriage of children is for parents. Many times parents are so blindfolded with their list of requirements, that they are not able to see the other side of that.

"Life is not about following blindly; it is about creating something meaningful. Why don't you people understand… marriage is not at all about making compromises. It is about love, understanding, compassion that both the partners share together. Love is love, despite any caste, creed, religion or gender."

She received a brainwave. True, love is love, it resides in the heart of a man or woman, who feel it for each other. Moments spent with Mitash and Enrique appeared in front of her eyes as the words she spoke struck her subconscious mind again and again.

"They both thought that by marrying someone you chose, they will make you all happy and when you would have enjoyed your share of happiness, they would have divorced and then mutually married the one whom they really loved and wanted as partners for their life.

"Would you have easily accepted it? How long would your happiness have existed? Bade Papa, Badi Mummy what is not good about Monica that you refused to make her your daughter-in-law? Is she less beautiful than Vinita? Is she or her family less educated than Vinita's? Of course not. She herself earns around two lakhs every month. A little more than Sanchit Bhaiya, honestly! The amount you received once from Vinita's family is approximately the same she would have brought to your family every year."

Everyone's mouth opened with a big O imagining the number of zeros Monica earns, including Sanchit's mom and dad.

"Vinita, I am sorry, I don't intend to embarrass you, but would you like to tell us how much you get every month?" Varushka asked.

"Err… forty thousand, per month," Vinita replied.

"But that girl does not belong to our caste. What will people say about it?" Sanchit's mom interrupted.

"What will they say if Vinita turns out to be the worst daughter-in-law who does not respect nor care for her in-laws. After all, she bought their son," Sanchit got his voice back in the debate. He winked at Vinita, mouthing a sorry.

His parents stared at him, looking embarrassed.

Vinita tried hard to hide her smile.

"You guys can't even imagine how difficult it was taking such a decision," Varushka wiped the tears rolling down the corner of her eyes. "When parents like you compel their children to marry someone else's child and have to suffer. The family suffers. All aspects of their life suffer. When someone elopes and gets married, then it hurts the family as well. I don't want them to meet my fate. So now you decide what you want to do? What actually could bring shame upon the family? Marriage at the end of the day is a necessity and not a compulsion."

"Hold on. What happened to you Varushka?" asked Sanchit's dad. A silence took over. Varushka had completely forgotten where she was and what exactly she had to say and what she was saying. Her mother came and hugged her to stop her emotions from overflowing.

Sanchit's dad looked at his younger brother and his wife when Varushka held her tongue. They too refused to answer, looking at the number of heads around watching them.

Sensing the air growing thick with tension again, Sanchit exploded another bomb. "She is married to someone who is already in a relationship with someone else and now they are getting divorced."

"I understand you are angry and you have a right to be, but if Vinita and I get married now, we are going to end up divorced, too. So you decide if you are going to be angry with us forever," Sanchit said for added effect.

Another round of tch-tch followed.

The elders then discussed things among themselves for fifteen minutes. Varushka's dad and uncle came forward to hug Varushka and Sanchit. And Vinita's mom and Sanchit's mom hugged Vinita. Everyone hugged everyone and there was a lot of hugging, crying, kissing and peace-making.

"Cancelling an engagement is better than getting into a bad marriage. What about all the arrangements we've made?" Vinita's dad asked thinking about the guests who were here to celebrate the auspicious occasion, besides the money already spent, and of course the bookings that couldn't be cancelled at this final moment.

"Well, we could still celebrate," Varushka said clearing her throat.

"Celebrate what?" Sanchit's mom asked.

"Are you ready to accept Monica as your daughter-in-law? And are you ready to accept Krishna as your son-in-law?" Varushka proposed to both the parents while Sanchit and Vinita were staring at her with no clue about the strategy Varushka was going to implement now.

They looked at each other and nodded 'yes' together.

"As both families have already met Monica, Krishna and their families, you can still complete the engagement function," Varushka said.

There was silence. Everyone looked confused, anxious and horrified, listening intently.

"I have talked to the hotel manager and they'll let us continue our function until evening. I have called Monica and Krishna, along with their parents. They've agreed and will be reaching here in a few minutes. So we would be having two engagement ceremonies together," she explained.

"But what about the rings, and other things?" Vinita's dad asked.

Rhea stretched out her right hand with two boxes of rings.

"This special engagement doesn't need anything more than blessings and good wishes from all of you," Vinita and Sanchit announced.

"And this calls for a celebration. We will return the money you have given to me and the money spent on this function will be shared," Sanchit's Dad said and everyone agreed.

The hall was soon filled with happy shrieks, hooting, clapping and cheers. The thickness in the air dissolved. The elders along with Sanchit and Vinita's parents praised the younger generation that they took the right decision and showed the light to the elders, setting examples for many others.

In the next forty minutes, a new to-be bride and a groom, Monica and Krishna entered. The entire family ran to welcome them and in time celebrations hit the floor.

Sanchit and Monica, Vinita and Krishna exchanged rings and the air began overflowing with happiness.

"My sisters, you really saved us all today," Sanchit said to Varushka halfway through the dancing. Vinita and Monica hugged Rhea and Varushka, the saviours of their love life.

"True love does come at a heavy price," Rhea smirked, offering Sanchit's credit card back to him.

"It has roughly cost you a lakh and thirty thousand rupees," Varushka added as they all burst into laughter.

"So where is my fee for making the impossible possible?" Varushka asked.

"Whatever and whenever you ask for," Sanchit replied as he kissed his younger sister's forehead.

Truth Prevails

"**I** can't believe you did that. What was the need to tell the crowd about your divorce? Thank god we managed to divert their minds back to the ongoing topic. You have no idea where the gossip about this will lead to. I am still not convinced by why you want a divorce," Varushka's mom said.

She had brought up the topic for the eleventh time since they had returned from the party.

"Mom, can we talk about this tomorrow?" Rhea said. She pulled a chair next to Varushka at the dining table. She tapped Varushka's thigh under the table in support. Varushka was all set to face the upcoming drama.

"Which couples don't fight? It does not mean that they end up in a divorce. If it keeps happening, there will be no married people around. Besides, what were you saying about parents compelling their children to marry? Didn't we ask you that time if you want to marry someone else? You denied it and so we started to look for a suitable boy for you. How is it wrong to see our children well settled? Tell me, how?" Varushka's mom began to weep.

Varushka prepared herself to speak, but her mom was in no mood to give her a chance.

"Look at us only, how much I fight with your Dad. Yet we have been together all the way since the last twenty-one years. Also, look at anyone in our family, relatives and neighbours – don't they fight and make up? It was good you saved Sanchit and those other two girls from a future possibility of divorce, but why are you bent on ruining your own life?" her mom continued.

Varushka was looking down with emotional heat building in her body, staring blankly at her dinner, quietly waiting and pleading in her mind for her mom to stop.

When her mom did stop, Varushka held eye contact with her Mom for few seconds, and then turned her glance towards Rhea and finally at her dad who had now joined them at the table. Rhea too had stopped eating, holding her head with her left hand and playing with her spoon with her right hand. Her eyes were fixed on the centre of the table.

"She is only asking for a divorce, not planning to commit suicide, Mom," Rhea interrupted her crying mother.

"Suicide would have been a better option than hurting us and yourself every moment," her mom raised her voice in hysteria.

"Are you serious? Now stop it! Don't take my silence as support," Varushka's dad slammed his fist on the table. "Mind your words while talking with our daughters."

Everyone froze and stared at him with wide eyes.

"Di, for god's sake, say something! Otherwise you'll be blamed for this for the rest of your life." Rhea whispered to Varushka. "I can't see someone who was a fighter in the morning act as a timid victim now," she added.

Varushka wondered why sometimes it was easy to fight and stand for others and difficult when you had to take a stand for yourself.

"I know what divorce means to you all. It was not easy to decide this, just like the decision about marriage. You only heard I want a divorce and you both started lecturing me. You didn't even bother to ask me what went wrong. Your presumptions and splitting hair won't work all the time. This world and life is not confined only to your family, relatives, neighbours and so-called society… there is much more happening," Varushka screamed.

She tried to hold back the seething avalanche of tears to wash away her anger.

"Is he having an affair with any girl there? Or was he already married to someone else?" her dad asked in a low tone, stroking her head.

"No, he did not marry anyone else," Varushka replied.

"Thank god. Then it is nothing much to worry about. He is married to you now. These kinds of love-shove issues are easily forgotten," her mom sniffed.

"Mom…" Varushka said rolling her eyes in exasperation.

"Today's generation won't even let you speak," her mom mumbled.

"And I expect your generation to behave more maturely," Varushka protested.

"Will you both please stop fighting like cats and dogs. Now you both keep your mouths shut and only the one I ask, will speak," her dad shouted. "Varushka, we are sorry, beta. These kind of things never ever happened in in our family for many generations. We find it difficult to accept such things. My child, please tell us what has happened between Mitash and you, and hopefully with our experience, we can both help you solve this."

Varushka now felt some sort of ease seeing someone ready to listen to her. She was still staring down, unable to find words, to begin with.

"Di, say something..." Rhea said bringing her back from her thoughts.

"Dad, Mom. I don't know how to say this. I don't know if you would understand me or not. You can't simply digest the thought of me getting a divorce. This marriage… is a lie. Simply an illusion."

Except for Rhea, they were looking at her perplexed, wondering what she was saying.

"Mitash is…" Varushka paused.

"Mitash, what?" her parents said together.

"I can't tell you right now. I need some time," Varushka said without looking at them.

There was a long silence.

"Varushka. I don't know what happened between you both or has his family said anything to you. Your Mom and I are really worried about you. We will wait for you to come and discuss your problems with us. We are your parents and always pray for your happiness. Before you make any conclusion, I simply want to suggest a few things to you, as a father and a friend. Ask yourself with all honesty, if you have put enough effort to make your marriage a success. Think realistically and review your expectations from your husband. Remember, time heals all wounds. Give some time to work things out with your husband if you can. No matter what kind of issues you face, know that there are a lot of other people who face bigger problems than yours. See yourself as a third person and see what you can do to save your marriage from dissolving. There is nothing like 'happily married forever' as we see in movies and fairy tales. No two people are the same or agree over the same things always.

"Further consider, what about your life after divorce? Life is not going to be easy. Once the 'divorced' stamp is put on you, you will have to be strong to handle every voice sniggering against you.

"My darling daughter, who will take care of you, if something happens to us? I rest my case, I know you are smart enough," her dad said in a concerned serious tone.

Varushka nodded, picked up her stuff and went to her room. She couldn't stop her flowing tears. Also, she was battling with what it was that was stopping her from telling her parents the obvious reason of her decision for separating from her husband of barely few months. She wasn't clear about her future too. She couldn't understand why her parents were worried about who'd take care of her.

The thoughts were now suffocating her.

She decided to check her mail to see if there was any response from Mitash. Lying in her bed, she opened her laptop. She had received two emails that caught her attention, among few junk emails. One was from Mitash and the other one was from Technesight HR. She decided to open the mail from Technesight first with the hope that it would give her some good news. Soon, she was proven wrong. She then clicked on the other mail that interested her. The one from Mitash. A long one.

Dear Varushka,

Thanks for sparing some time to finally read the emails I sent and replying.

I don't know where to start. Okay, let me start by saying that I'm truly sorry!

I know I've said it probably a million times, but I feel like I need to keep apologizing. I keep saying it in the hope that you'll understand all the things I'm apologizing for. I'm sorry that all the memories we made are now tainted with sadness. I'm sorry that I couldn't really explain to you why it all happened. I'm sorry I hurt you, I broke your heart. I'm just so INCREDIBLY SORRY.

I still remember the moment you came to know about Enrique and my relationship. I saw it all in your eyes – betrayal, disillusionment, revulsion. At that moment, I just wanted to crawl under a rock somewhere and hide. Now that I understand the gravity of what I've done. My actions have filled me with self-loathing and remorse. It's difficult for me to look in the mirror and I'm not proud of the man I see when I do.

I never wanted to manipulate or hurt you.

You might not believe me, you probably won't believe me, but you breaking up with me was the hardest thing I've ever had to face. It hurt me hurting you. It's never easy hurting someone you love and I do, I love you. You didn't ask and I didn't tell you, but here's the truth: I love you as my closest confidant. I really love you as my family and your happiness means a lot to me.

In the past few months, we've become so much a part of each other's lives that I really can't imagine my life without you anymore. I don't think divorce would benefit either one of us to give up on this relationship. Life is not as simple as we wish it to be. The world is not as supportive.

Think once, we have invested ourselves so much into this relationship already and our good times have far outnumbered the bad. Our life was running smoothly. Our family was living happily and peacefully. This one step would stir the life around us. Society and family will make us marry someone else. Being a man, it won't be so much of a difficulty for me, but it is not going to be easy for you, leading a life after getting labelled as a divorced woman. Moreover, we are not alone. Do think about Rhea and Shrini. Would it be easy for them afterwards to walk ahead when all the eyes would see them with suspicion? No. Never.

If I accept my sexuality in front of the society, would they allow Shrini and my parents to even breathe or sleep peacefully?

You are my closest friend, my best friend. I don't know when it happened, I don't know how and I don't know how my feelings for you changed and I fell in love, deeply, with this connection with you. I felt the harmony of my family of three – Enrique, you and me – as so perfect and complete. It's not your fault, it's not my fault and it's not Enrique's fault either. The sand in our hourglass just ran out. I was scared of losing you, and that stopped me from telling you the truth.

I gave my best to be the kind of husband that I felt you deserved. A nice kind man you could trust, the kind you could feel proud of, the kind who would fulfil all your wishes and dreams. Enrique, despite the torture for him daily, supported me all the way. I know I have hurt him as well, a lot. It was not easy for him either, to accept the third person in my life. But, when you came into our lives, even he adjusted and felt my completeness.

I have no excuse for what happened and my saying 'I'm sorry' hardly seems adequate. If you could forgive me, I promise I will as always put you first to achieve your aspirations in your charted path to success.

We three would happily pick up where we left off, just doing everyday things like coming back to the apartment after work, kicking back on the couch and sharing the ups and downs of each other's day. I would enjoy taking turns at being chef and appreciate Enrique's and your willingness to watch a game with me once in a while. I had already started to plan our next vacation together before this happened. Wouldn't it be great if we could still get away together for a while and put this behind us?

I know I'm really expecting a lot from you to continue making plans with me, but the alternative is too painful to even consider. Please remember all the good times we had already, as well as all the good times that are still out there, waiting for us to discover.

If not as husband and wife, as best friends, without the legal separation. Think about it…

Yours,

Mitash

Varushka was feeling exhausted to think about anything, after reading the hopeless mail for the second time. Her eyelashes felt heavy with stress, and she couldn't prevent them from closing.

The Divorce Notice

Either a wedding or the build-up towards the divorce, can't ever happen without relatives being in the dark. In films and novels, the most difficult and challenging thing for lovers is to convince their parents to allow them to marry. However, it's a hurricane when a person takes a stand to get a divorce. The whole society joins in as protest.

Well, Varushka planning to divorce her husband was clearly entrenched into everyone's mind at Sanchit's engagement. By next morning, the news had spread like wildfire.

Every few minutes, Varushka's mom and dad's phones were ringing, receiving calls from relatives from all corners of the world. This continued for the next few days. It was really making the whole family depressed and uncomfortable.

Once the news finally got out about the divorce, Varushka noticed that people tended to react in one of two ways; they either wanted to pity her or they wanted to use her situation to denounce the divorce trend among the young generation. Varushka wanted no part in either situation.

She called Ritvik for his suggestion, informing him about the mail she received from Mitash.

Ritivik was clear, "It means he is not ready to sign the divorce papers."

Varushka agreed, "I guess, we can assume that."

"But he has got a point about the life after divorce being difficult for the families too," Ritvik said softly.

"Are you refusing to help me?"

Ritvik quickly clarified, "I didn't mean that. It is my profession, I can't say no to the money coming. But as you came to me with my sister's reference to Rhea, I am making you aware of the possible future events. I have seen many cases, you know.

"Hmmm. So what is your advice, Mr Lawyer?" she asked.

"Wait for some time and try to convince Mitash for a mutual divorce. Meanwhile, you better find a job. It would certainly empower you, bringing back your confidence. Your parents and you would be able to handle the situation more positively then. Trust me, the real empowerment comes from being financially independent. Then I can double my fees by charging you for career consultation too," he said encouraging her, finishing off with light laughter.

They both laughed, Varushka after a long time.

For the next two weeks, hundreds of emails were exchanged between Mitash and Varushka. Varushka kept trying to convince Mitash for a divorce, and he didn't give up pleading to not divorce him as an option.

Mails have a benefit over calls, at least one isn't able to disconnect the conversation in between and the other one gets an opportunity to explain everything he or she has. Besides, they don't have to react instantly; one can take as much time needed before sending a detailed reply. The emotions reflected in the voice are always a threat to manipulate the other.

In the interim, her family kept trying to ask her the reason why she left Mitash, whereas, she kept trying hard to avoid encountering her parents' badgering. Everything felt a lot harder to deal with. Sometimes she felt like running away, far away from everyone who knew her or whom she knew.

Most of the time, Varushka occupied herself in composing emails to Mitash and to HRs or sleeping.

Among all the negativity around her, one good thing happened. Varushka had performed extraordinarily during her studies at the Amsterdam University. She was still on leave, however, the university management decided to allow her to complete her course online. This gave her hope that things would change in her favour.

"Di, why are you being so obstinate? What are you trying to do by hiding the truth from mom and dad? Don't you think they'd be on your side with you and would immediately send a notice to your in-laws," Rhea tried to persuade her sister.

Varushka didn't answer.

"Hey! I am talking to you," Rhea snatched the magazine Varushka was reading. "Have you seen your face recently? It looks so pale and sullen. Your eyes are gloomy and surrounded by dark circles with bags under them. What are you even trying to do? Just stop pretending to be a 'Powerpuff Girl' who'll handle everything on her own."

"Then what should I do? Tell them the guy you chose as my life partner is gay. Blame them for the wrong and worst decision ever they have made by ruining their daughter's life?" Varushka said staring the blank wall in front of her. "Will they be able to handle it at this age, when they have done a lot for us, for our happiness? Would it be easy for you after that? Would anyone marry Shrini when people in our society come to know that her brother got divorced because he is gay and his family hid the dark truth from everyone?"

Rhea thought for few seconds. She did not have an answer.

"But what about you?" she asked.

"I don't know," Varushka replied with no noticeable enthusiasm.

Do I have the courage to follow my heart or do I have to make a choice, once again for the happiness of two families, she wondered.

An Unexpected Twist

Varushka stepped out of her room after thirty-six hours and looked around.

Rhea was watching a travel channel and their dad was giving her company. Her mom was chopping *bhindi* and onions for dinner.

"Di…" Rhea grinned in surprise. Her Mom and Dad relaxed on seeing her up and about. The normally tensed air seemed to trickle away with positivity welcoming the change with a smile.

"How are you feeling honey?" her mom asked.

"I am okay," Varushka replied, keeping her tone even. "I want to talk to you all."

"Come, sit here," her mom requested.

Rhea tried to read her sister's mind.

"What happened? You wanted to say something na?" Dad said when Varushka didn't speak in the next minute.

"I'm sorry. I'm sorry that I hurt you both a lot in the past few months. It was not that I never thought about it, it was not that I didn't try to give it my best, it was never that I didn't think about you both. I was so disturbed inside that I couldn't even imagine the possibility of any other solution.

"Neither was it easy for me to take such a step. I read a lot about it, thought a lot, explored everything. Even met a lawyer lately, everything was fixed. However, I do not want to hurt you all. I can't hurt my family anymore. I've decided to give up. To give up, once more."

Her parents along with Rhea looked at Varushka and then at each other, perplexed.

"I'm not going to divorce Mitash," she declared.

Her Mom was so overwhelmed by her words that she got up, walked to her and gave her a tight crushing hug.

"Thank you," she whispered with tears of joy rolling down her eyes.

Varushka feebly hugged her back.

Rhea was shocked and disappointed at the decision made by Varushka. Her Dad was sitting still.

"Aren't you happy, Dad?" Varushka asked noticing him.

"Absolutely, I am. But curiosity is pricking me inside. At least now you can tell us what you were trying to hide from us all this time," he said.

"I will. Today I will tell you everything. But there is one thing to say before that," Varushka said.

Everyone looked at her, holding their breath, it seemed.

"I'm not divorcing him. Nor am I going to stay with him. I've got a job offer in Germany," Varushka said, looking at her sister who was not happy like her parents about her previous announcement.

She continued, "I know you are not happy with me, but I hope you will be fine after listening to what I am going to tell you now. I agree that you both have burnt the midnight oil to give every possible happiness to Rhea and me. You provided us with the best food, best clothing, toys, education and every other thing that could have been possibly done, and even more. I know, being a parent you feel the marriages of your children is one of the biggest responsibilities and you tried your best to find the perfect life partner for me. You did your part, impeccably, and I mean it.

"Ultimately, it was not you. Rather, it was me who made the final call of marrying Mitash. I married him, happily. Went to start a new family of my own, like yours. I started understanding my new life, my dreams, and my family. Life was phenomenal. You know, I even joined a university there. I was exploring many new things. I was madly in love with my life. Then again, nothing is perfect in this world.

"One day, suddenly, my universe turned upside down when I came to know Mitash is not like us. He is gay, already in a relationship with another man, who was also living with us. My marriage, my beliefs, my faith turned out to be an illusion." She just kept talking, not daring to look at her parents, scared of seeing their reaction now.

"I went numb, my mind stopped responding properly. The only unilateral decision I could have made was to come back to you – my parents, my family, my sense of my true home.

"Lately, I realized it was not Enrique who was living with us, but it was me who entered his home, his life. He was the one who was sacrificing and sharing his love, the most difficult decision one could ever make. I can't do that. I can't live with someone who is someone else's love. I can't share the same roof with him, only for the sake of being known as a married woman.

"So now I have decided, I will prefer a separation, rather than a legal divorce. This will maintain the peace in both the families and society."

Varushka exhaled heavily and stopped.

Her dad was the first one to finally break the sombre silence that had enveloped the living room after her long monologue.

"But why didn't you tell us anything till now, beta? Why, Varushka?" he sobbed. And then he came and hugged her really tight. "My daughter was in so much pain, handling this all alone. And we were not aware of it at all."

The pain of realizing oneself as a failed parent is the worst feeling for parents. It is a catastrophic moment for them.

"What is this? Any new disease?" her Mom asked looking at all of them. "Would anyone explain it to me as well? What is this gay-shay thing?"

Well, now it was a tricky thing to explain the term when two generations were together.

Rhea, Varushka and their dad couldn't resist chuckling in that distressing milieu.

"What Fawad Khan was as Rahul Kapoor in the movie *Kapoor and Sons*," Dad said after thinking for a second, with the hope that his wife would understand.

"You remember, I asked you at that time also. You promised to explain it to me once we came back home, but you never did," her mom complained.

Rhea thought of giving it a try. "Have you seen the movie *Dostana*, Mom?" she questioned.

"Naah!" her mom replied.

Rhea looked at her Dad, he looked back at her. Both shook their head in dismay.

"You must have heard, at least about a man marrying another man or a girl marrying another girl?" Varushka asked.

"Oh, god! Does it happen in reality?" It was a big-time shock for their mother.

"I don't know. I too had seen it in movies and read it in the news," their Dad added.

"I also have read lots of such stories about the LGBTQ community and they do have support groups and NGOs as well," added Rhea.

"Now what is this LGBTQ?" their mom clearly had no clue about this.

"LGBTQ is the short form for Lesbian, Gay, Bisexual, Transgender and Queer. In fact, one of my friends was telling me that one of his cousins is also an out of the closet proud gay man," Rhea updated everyone with this latest news.

"Really?" said her parents in unison, their brows creased.

"Yes! And now we are hearing this about Mitash Jiju."

For another hour, everyone was enlightening everyone with the details they had and the other evidence and statics they discovered from different media to educate in offering clarity to their mom, besides each other.

"We can't let you be in this trap anymore. My daughter deserves a true husband, a happy married life. I will not leave them, nor forgive them easily. How could one play with another's emotions, dreams and life? Varushka, my poor darling child, you don't worry. Your dad is with you. I will find a lawyer and send them a notice as soon as possible."

Finally, there was a positive twist in the family drama. Rhea was loving it.

"But Dad, when the news of the reason for my divorce floats out, how will you handle it? Will these people accept Mitash, after knowing about his orientation? What will happen to Shrini?" Varushka put across her concern.

"Do you think your Dad is too weak to handle other people's opinions that really don't matter?" her dad asked.

"He is absolutely right." Varushka's mom supported him. "Call them right away."

"No! I will now see them in court, directly," he proclaimed.

Varushka and Rhea were surprised with this sudden transformation of their parents, ready to support their children without caring about public opinion.

The Impossible Happened

It was nearly 9 a.m. when Varushka woke up on Sunday morning a couple of days later. The house seemed to be in panic mode. She didn't quite know what was going on or even if there was something going on, but even from her door-locked bedroom, she could feel there was a sense of unrest in the air. She sat up on her bed. Her head felt heavier. She held her head for a while and surveyed the scene. The room looked exactly the way it did the previous night. Outside the room, she could hear the sound of footsteps pacing hastily back and forth.

"What now?" she wondered as she threw her blanket aside and got out of bed.

Varushka was in a state of shock seeing the chaos outside.

"*Rheaa! Mom! Dad!*" she called, but there was no answer. She scanned the house but found nobody around. She noticed the main gate outside was open. She rushed towards the door. She found Rhea crying, looking at their parents driving away in their Honda City. One neighbour was consoling her.

"Rhea. What happened? Where are Mom and Dad going?" Varushka screamed in panic.

"Mom woke up with severe chest pain. Dad's taking her to the hospital," Rhea managed to reply.

"Which hospital? But why didn't anyone wake me up?" Varushka asked shaking her sister.

"Heart Hospital. Dad said you came very late from Bangalore last night and asked me not to disturb you," Rhea answered looking away.

Varushka grimaced. "I am going to the hospital, are you coming?" she said and ran to her room.

She swiftly pulled off her pyjamas and slipped on her black jeans. She washed her face with water, patted it dry with a towel, wrapped the first scarf she found around her neck, picked up her jacket, mobile, wallet and car keys.

"How did this happen? So early in the morning?" Varushka asked Rhea, as she drove them to the hospital.

Rhea was silent.

"Speak up, goddammit." Varushka shouted angrily at Rhea. She felt her feet shaking, losing the grip on the pedal for a second.

"Shrini and her mother came over this morning. Seems they have received the legal notice yesterday late evening," Rhea answered softly.

"Legal notice?" Varushka mumbled.

"For your divorce," Rhea answered.

"Oh my god. When did this happen? Have you read it? What does it say?" Varushka enquired.

"Di… Be careful…" For the first time, Rhea was scared of her sister's driving at this time.

Varushka changed the gear, slowing down the car.

"Dad asked me if I knew the lawyer you had met and I told them about Ritvik Bhaiya. The day you left for Bangalore for your meeting with that German company head, Dad called him home. They discussed a lot about the consequences and the best possible way out. Ritvik suggested not to mention in the notice about Mitash being gay as they might deny the fact. Proving the same would not be easy, which might lead to embarrassment for you as well. Dad and Mom were ready to agree for anything that will bring you out of this ambush without bringing your name getting tainted."

Varushka just looked ahead and drove, so Rhea added, "Trust me, Di. I can bet that Shrini's mom knows everything about Mitash Jiju."

Varushka was listening silently, balancing her focus between driving and Rhea's narration. She parked the car at the parking lot, stepped down and ran inside the hospital.

"Call Dad and ask where he is," Varushka instructed.

Rhea called thrice, but her call was not received. "Let me check at the reception," she said.

Varushka scanned the space around. Their dad was nowhere to be seen.

"Mom is in the ICU!" Rhea shouted in a gasping voice. The word ICU scared the hell out of her.

Both the sisters ran in the direction the signboard instructed.

They found their Dad pacing in the corridor restlessly, outside the ICU.

"Dad, how's Mom? Is she alright? Why is she in the ICU?" Varushka asked anxiously.

"The doctors haven't confirmed anything," Dad replied, followed by a choked breath from his lungs, and suddenly he leaned over the bench nearby. Rhea ran and held him. His strength left him, even as he attempted to stand. Varushka fetched a glass of water for him.

Varushka called Sanchit, briefing him about the scenario, and asked him to come to the hospital or send Bade Papa at the earliest. Extended family support is de rigueur in such a crucial situation when all those present in the hospital were feeling unnerved.

Varushka harked back at Rhea to tell her about the morning incident. "So, what happened after that?" she asked exasperated. "In the morning…" Varushka added spotting Rhea's baffled look.

"Today morning, at seven, the doorbell rang. I had just woken up and was making my tea. Dad opened the door and out of curiosity, I peeped through the curtains outside the kitchen. Everyone was shocked to see Shrini with her mother. Apparently Mitash's father is away on a business trip to Australia.

"Aunty screamed even before entering the house, 'How dare you send those papers to my house blaming my son and my family?' It was really an awkward moment with our neighbours around.

"Dad requested her to come inside and then say whatever she wished to. She refused his request and began to blame you and our family. She was angry that he hadn't called them before taking any such step. It made Dad furious and he accused her of hiding the fact that she and her son were playing with you and our family emotions. However, she was not ready to accept it.

"You know how our neighbours are. In front of everyone, she cruelly incited that you eloped from Amsterdam as you had an affair with someone there and now were blaming her son and family with the intention to claim the money we spent on the wedding and the dowry.

"Mom couldn't take it and collapsed on the sofa, complaining of severe chest pain. Dad didn't want you to face Aunty, so we didn't wake you when she came and after that, there was utter chaos. Thankfully someone ran and called the doctor next to our house. He gave Mom emergency first aid and by that time Dad got ready to head to the hospital.

"Sensing the gravity of the situation, Aunty asked Shrini to drive them back home. However, seeing Mom's condition, Shrini offered to help, but her mother didn't allow her to go ahead. They went back.

"Di, the scene has turned the real dirty now. If she wasn't aware of the reality, she would have checked with Mitash Jiju about what went wrong. Was she not aware since the last few months that you have come back to us?" Rhea expressed her doubts.

Varushka hid her face with her palms, then slid them over her head, down to the back of her neck. She gasped for some air. She couldn't understand what to do. She looked up, stood there for a while, then walked towards her dad. She sat next to him, rested her head on his lap closing her eyes.

"I am sorry, Dad. I screwed up everything," she said. Dad felt a tear drop roll down from her eyes and wiped it off, taking a deep breath. Putting on a fake smile, he said, "It's not your fault. Somewhere, we too are responsible for this day. We were over enthusiastic about you getting married. We were satisfied to see what was easily visible to us and never tried to see the other side. God is punishing us for our deeds."

"God cannot be so cruel that he'll harm our family anymore," Varushka said, with her head on her dad's lap.

▼

Sanchit arrived at the hospital along with his parents to offer strength and solace to his sisters and uncle. Rhea rushed to receive them along with Varushka. There were reassuring hugs and hellos. Somberness swathed the ambience.

Hours had passed by, and a crowd had gathered at the hospital – Bua, Mama, Mami, two other aunties, uncles and a few cousins joined to lend succour and express sympathy.

"How did this happen so suddenly?" Sanchit's dad asked.

Varushka's dad turned his face towards Varushka and looked away with discontentment. He briefed them about Mitash's mom's arrival in the morning and the following drama.

"Awful. We didn't give much attention to her words that day on Sanchit's engagement," Sanchit's dad said in a quiet and calm voice. "It means, she was saying all that genuinely?"

The incident during Sanchit's engagement had really changed his approach.

"Varushka is getting a divorce?" Bua shrieked. "Is this some kind of a joke?"

Her eyes were pleading with Varushka to tell her it was a joke and that they were playing the fool.

"No one is joking, we are serious," Rhea replied.

There was a stunned silence in the hall after that. It was as though someone had thrown a bombshell and the family was reeling in the aftermath of the rubble that the explosion had left.

"But, what's the matter?" Sanchit's mom asked. She was shocked as were others.

"How many days has she been married? Barely five months!" Mami proclaimed. Everyone else nodded.

Varushka looked at her dad and pleaded to him not to speak.

Rhea noticed this silent conversation between her father and sister. She was now boiling with rage.

"Enough Di. They do not care about either our family or you. Today Mom collapsed in front of Mitash's mother, what did she do? Simply walked away. Our mother is in the ICU and you still care about him and the honour of his family. Don't you even know how she behaved in front of all our neighbours, how she showed you in a bad light? Enough is enough."

Rhea turned to her uncle and recited the whole story she knew till now.

Everyone was jolted by another atomic bomb. Although, the elder ladies and few of the men could not understand what was wrong with Mitash's character.

"Is he suffering from any hi-fi disease?" Bua asked.

Sanchit rolled his eyes. "I have heard and seen it in movies. I never believed it more than any fiction or fantasy," he said, sadly.

"And if he is gay, what is the need for a divorce? I mean, we can consult doctors and psychiatrists to cure him," Mami suggested.

"See, your parents have had to spend lakhs of money over this wedding and on top of that, gave a huge dowry too. Do you want to waste this big amount of money and put it in the dustbin for newly found freedom?" Mama Ji asked Varushka.

"And what next? She has to marry someone again and now you would have to waste your retirement savings for taking such a stupid decision for such silly issues," continued Mama Ji, now looking at Varushka's dad.

With exasperation another uncle added, "That's why we don't suggest higher education for girls. They tend to become intolerant and don't even care to save their marriage or family's face."

In the other corner, Varushka was silently listening to them, with no zest to answer them, nor any zeal to protest. 'The problem they are considering silly is not just silly. But much larger than their thoughts,' she thought.

Just then, Dr Kunal Verma, the head of cardiology stepped of the ICU beaming and put his hand on Varushka's father saying, "Mr Jha, I am happy to say that your wife's condition has now stablised. We are moving her to her allotted room for observation overnight. You should be proud because your timely action averted a major heart-attack. My conclusions observe the condition was brought on by an excessive stress attack. When discharged, I suggest at home, you see to her comfort and rest for the next ten days. Thereafter, please bring her over to meet me for a final check-up. I will sign her discharge papers for tomorrow morning as I am confident she is recovering well."

"Thank you! Thank you, Doctor," Varushka's dad emotionally replied holding Dr Verma's hands.

▼

Three days later, after Varushka's mom was home recovering, Varushka was shaken out of her thoughts when her phone buzzed. It was Ritvik.

"Did you see the news, Varushka?" he enquired urgently.

"Aah, no. What happened?" she replied with curiosity.

"Fast, go and turn on your television," he commanded.

"But Ritvik, I am making lunch for the family," she replied, softly. "Is it really important for me to see it now?"

"You better put on the TV *right now*!" he ordered.

The family was watching a daily soap, but Varushka pleaded urgently, "Ritvik has asked us to watch a national news channel right now. Something very very important is on."

Her family gazed at her in surprise, trying to comprehend her urgency.

"What happened? Anything serious?" Sanchit asked.

"Ritvik, my lawyer, is asking me to watch any national news channel right away," she said looking at Rhea and then at her father.

In no time, Rhea took the remote control and flipped to a news channel.

The news anchor was reporting about a video that had gone viral globally in an hour and was everywhere over the internet and electronic media. Varushka turned pale and ashen, taken aback with shock. It was Mitash in the news. She went near the television, to absorb what she saw and heard clearly. Her shocked family, murmuring aloud, became more audible than the television. Rhea increased the volume to subside their voices.

Namaste India, meri matra bhoomi, main kaun? Main yahaan kyun?

I am your escaped criminal, your gaandu, your hijra, chhaka, namard... aur naam dena hain to dijiya kyunki, I have run far away and now maybe forever... India, you promote 377, you suffocate every breath of mine. I tried to be honest, but you choked me to not letting me love and be loved freely. I was born into a Brahmin family, studied all the scriptures to understand and see the depictions in writing and art of god's expression of love amongst two consenting adults.

I'm not brave and I have seen that whoever has tried to be honest, has been hung or criminalized or has even committed suicide. There are many like me, crushed and married, spoiling two lives and two families. Be informed, I am not the carrier of AIDS, I'm not a paedophile who needs medical treatment. I am a gay man who loves an adult man, who knew how he was differently inclined even when he was in school. It was also the period I realized and immensely feared that being myself was against the law. I hated myself for being unable to control myself and my feelings. I hated everyone around me. That time for me was claustrophobic. I have cried in the bathroom in my helplessness. There was no one I could talk to or who would understand how I felt. That was the time I was on the verge of depression, contemplating suicide at the fate for people inclined towards the same sex like me.

I am someone who explored this in puberty and honestly the toughest person to convince that I am gay was me. Once I had found a way to accept myself, I found my true inner peace. I was then lucky to convince my new agenda by cheating my parents after researching how easy it was to be myself out of India by pursuing further education and building my future far away from my family and their society in India, that was hell bent on controlling my freedom. Unfortunately, in this journey, I have terribly hurt and wronged people who nurture and care for me. I will take my part of the blame, will you all?

Varushka, my lawfully wedded wife, I am your exploiter. I have played with your senses as that's the only way I knew I could keep my family honour in India. As much as you didn't deserve this, neither did I deserve our Indian society's beliefs and demands that compelled me to manipulate you. I thought by buying your dreams, I would keep you happy, as women are not a forefront in India. Thanks to my sister Shrini, I have gathered the courage to voice my extreme sense of sorrow and apology for whatever you are going through. Varushka, in spite of the shame of a failed marriage, you tried your best to keep my orientation and your hurt a secret. You will no longer have to… you are an honourable, genuine, good and supportive wife. From one human to another, I will stand by any decision of yours to move ahead to a better life. Enrique and I are ready to be your support if you are comfortable to reach the goals you have sacrificed. I will forever be indebted to you for giving me your precious life, to keep up my life.

Enrique, you have and always will be my love and soul mate. Your unquestionable and unlimited sacrifice and generosity in love for me and support to my wife and our families through all your emotional torment has made me strong to accept the truth and face up to this huge mistake today without you even saying "I told you so". The pain you have gone through with the façade I enacted towards Varuksha, covered with your fake smile or a double meaning joke to convert your pain has made me ashamed. Enrique, I know you will support me through all this as you are my soul spouse and you are there for me in good times and in bad. All I want now is to give you back a lifetime of happiness you truly deserve from me.

I cannot be asked to be given forgiveness as no one is to blame except society for its ignorance. I will, however, use my right to say sorry for the hurt that I have caused being a coward and not standing up and fighting for who I am. My family, inspite of me being honest about my love for Enrique, rejected my truth as loneliness that comes from living in a foreign country and a phase many lonely men explore before marriage. They believe that I will understand and prove my masculinity to myself as a real man by marrying a girl.

Varushka, being my best friend and unfortunate victim, has taught me honesty in life and now I believe real men face the truth head on and work through all that comes their way with bravery.

I will forgive my parents for first not being my family, but society. I will forgive Varuksha's family for not safeguarding her interests and crushing her aspirations and marrying her to a man who they never knew nor desired to find out completely about, as they thought she'd lose out on a rich suitor. So I plead forgiveness from the little goodness in my heart to my victims Varuksha and Enrique.

Walking Down the Aisle

A year later

It is a beautiful April day. The air is crisp and cool and the canal banks are lined with vibrant clouds of orange and red trees, besides a golden carpet of crunchy leaves.

"Come, come Rhea!" Mitash's mom dazzled in a cobalt blue georgette saree. "Where is Varushka?"

They were at The Arendshoeve, a famous garden in Amsterdam. A wedding was in progress.

Unlike Indian weddings, especially weddings of North India, there was a silence other than occasional whispering of the guests.

Finally, a celebrant came out and asked everyone to stand. The flower girls lined the path with lavender and fuschia rose petals as the music started playing John Paul Young's 'Love is in the air'.

All of a sudden, there was a shriek of happiness. Everyone turned their faces to the entrance.

In a lavender chiffon gown elegantly floating out around, her hair piled loosely on top of her head, stunning Varushka walked arm-in-arm, escorting Mitash down the aisle.

As they took two steps out, Mitash looked at Varushka. "You look absolutely beautiful," he said beaming proudly at her. Her cheeks and lips quirked upwards in a warm loving smile. She turned to him and looked piercingly with love into his eyes. "And I can't keep my eyes off you, debonair," she said, winking at him flirtingly.

All eyes were on the duo, taking their pictures, waving at them and smiling along with a few brown, black, green and blue eyes filled with tears.

"Ready to get this show on?" Varushka asked as she lightly nudged him.

He nodded. "I am surprised at the butterflies in my stomach – a mixture of excitement and nerves. I have been looking forward to this day for months and now that it is finally here, everything feels like a dream."

Up ahead at the altar with picturesque roman pillars behind, a smiling Enrique was patiently waiting for them.

Mitash's dark eyes were shining with happiness. "Oh my god, this is finally happening. I can't believe this is finally happening. This is like a dream. Is this for real? For real?"

"For real, for real," Varushka repeated pulling him slightly closer, clearly very thrilled too. Mitash also detected a tinge of tears at the corner of her eyes, tears of joy at his dream being fulfilled.

Varushka then held his right hand in her palms. He felt the warmth. She gave Mitash's hand to Enrique. Then suddenly she jerked it back. Everyone exclaimed 'Oh!' in shock. Whispering replaced the music around. Mitash and Enrique looked at her, a tad surprised.

Varushka looked back haughtily and proclaimed. "By the way, now I got the answer about why you both had put three coins in the Trevi Fountain and never explained it to me." And then breaking into a naughty wicked smile, she continued, "Relax, my darling men! I am not going to snatch your love away again." She immediately burst into laughter. The grooms and the guests joined the chortle.

Mitash pulled Varushka and Enrique in a hug. "Oh, Varushka, I am so happy. Thank you so much! For making all this happen!"

Varushka pulled back and looked at him. "This is so exciting. I told you it was going to happen. I can't tell you how glad I am being a part of this."

"You have changed my life," Mitash said.

"No, I didn't. You did. You're here because of everything you have done. I am proud that you have accepted and faced your truth," said Varushka and then she presented him to Enrique. "His hand would be yours to hold forever," Varushka placed his hand in Enrique's once again and smiled. "This time, forever. Hurt him and deck you to the ground."

She laughed as Ritvik came from behind, put his arm around her waist, and directed her to their seats.

Now, as a couple, Mitash and Enrique stood in front of the celebrant and all present.

Mitash's mind flashed back to his wanting to marry in India. Varushka and Mitash had approached many priests and religious institutions to bless his union with Enrique. Unfortunately, they were shunned, being told that they didn't want to conduct such a wedding as it was illegal in India. Varushka then comforted

Mitash, saying, "Don't get upset by these hypocrites. They happily and proudly perform weddings that have dowry, which is also illegal. Don't worry, it's my responsibility to see that your wedding takes place in Amsterdam."

Tears welled up in Mitash's eyes by the time vows were exchanged, followed by the exchange of the rings. Mitash and Enrique kissed each other deeply as a happily married couple.

▼

Before Varushka walked away, she hugged Enrique and Mitash once again, as happily divorced.

Epilogue

Mitash accepted the fact that he was gay, publically, via his video that had gone viral in a few minutes. His parents were not left with any other choice than asking Varushka and her family to forgive them and find the best way to amicably proceed and close the case against them. Mitash came down to India and he and Varushka got mutually divorced with the help of Ritvik.

Varushka trusted her passions, values and beliefs and she got through the crisis. She overcame a very confusing and unique divorce. It is truly said that after every storm comes the calm. You put behind your hurdles, learning through it and managing to survive much better. One thing is certain, when you sail out of a storm, you won't be the same person who walked in. That's what the storm was all about – an experience, a lesson to be learnt.

She forgave Mitash and was living in Germany. She occasionally visited Mitash and Enrique in Amsterdam or sometimes, they visited her in Frankfurt or sometimes they all travelled together like before. But the relation equation has changed. It has become honest with mutual respect.

It took almost a year for Varushka to convince Mitash's family to agree to their son's marriage to Enrique. Finally they agreed to accept Enrique as their son-in-law and in time, know understand and respect them both.

Shrini went to the US for her higher studies in Psychology. Rhea started working as a Research and Development specialist at a leading company in Bangalore.